Search for the White Moon

Natalie London

Search for the White Moon

Natalie London

Affinity
eBook Press
NZ
2016

Search for the White Moon
© 2016 by Natalie London

Affinity E-Book Press NZ LTD.
Canterbury, New Zealand

1st Edition

ISBN: 978-0-908351-65-7

Editor: Angela Koenig
Proof Editor: Alexis Smith
Cover Design: Irish Dragon Designs

Acknowledgments

All my thanks to Julie, Mel, Mary, Nancy, Angela Koenig, and the team at Affinity for their valuable assistance, and for sharing their knowledge and support. I am proud to be a part of the Affinity family.

Dedication

For Katherine B.

Table of Contents

Prologue

The rain beat down on the car, the wind blowing sheets of water against the windshield. She leaned forward, straining to see ahead in the darkness, the car's headlights throwing a faint beam of light that barely illuminated the narrow winding road.

With her hands gripping the unfamiliar steering wheel, she cautiously slowed for the next curve. It had been years since she had driven and months since her last trip away from the farm. Long before they started living there it had been a real working farm, but now the closest it came to having live animals were the cats and dogs.

For a fleeting second she wondered if they had discovered that the car was missing and she was gone. All she wanted was to get to town and find a telephone. Ahead, the road descended steeply before curving to the left with a drop-off on the right side.

Her eyes tracked to the rearview mirror where two bright headlights were approaching rapidly. The closer the vehicle got the more blinding the glare became. She knew there was some way to adjust the mirror, but it would be too dangerous to take her hands from the steering wheel.

The car picked up speed on the rapid descent and a curve loomed ahead. The lights in the mirror were now so close they were blinding her, and when she looked back at the road, she realized that she was going too fast for the curve. She slammed hard on the brakes and knew something was wrong as the brake pedal sank slowly to the car's floor. Unable to stop, the car picked up more speed going into the curve. The windshield wipers flapped back and forth, too slow to keep up with the driving rain, and she pulled at the steering wheel desperately, trying to keep the car on the road.

As the car left the road and sailed silently through the air. all she could think of was who would report the horrible plans she had overheard at the farm? Her vehicle hit the side of the hill, tumbled over, landed with a crashing grind of metal, and burst into flames. The truck behind her drove on.

Several motorists came upon the wreckage and leaped from their cars to gaze down the hill in speechless horror as flames soared upward. Someone yelled "Call 911" as the burning vehicle exploded. The wailing of sirens filled the rainy night, but by the time the fire trucks and rescue squad arrived, the car was only a crumpled, charred object with black smoke drifting toward the sky.

Chapter One

I skipped down the sidewalk. Well, not literally. The sight of a thirty-two-year-old woman skipping down the street would have been unusual, even here in New York City. Emotionally I felt like skipping. It was my day off work and I had gone for a long run in the crisp, sunny, December morning. Now I was on my way to the agency that had summoned me the day before, wondering what job was awaiting me.

I arrived in the warehouse district and looked at a large, old building with a sooty brick exterior and peeling paint trim that had an air of neglect and abandonment. A faded sign in the window read Atlantic Employment Agency. I climbed the concrete stairs and opened the large glass-plated door. Inside, the waiting room consisted of five scuffed-vinyl chairs arranged along two walls, and a battered end table piled with tattered old magazines. The floor, covered with dirty worn linoleum in a dreary specked pattern, had definitely seen better days. I sat down and picked up a magazine that featured an article on the spring fashions of five years ago. Anyone coming here looking for a job would find only a few offerings, usually not matched to the applicant's skills, and if pursued, never resulting in an offer of employment. No one ever recommended the agency and since it did not advertise, few people ventured here.

The receptionist, sitting behind the high counter and dressed in a plain white blouse and black skirt, with brown hair in a grown-out perm—the kind of person no one could later describe—nodded in my direction.

"You can go in now," she said, without making eye contact.

†

I went through the door to the right of her desk and walked down the dimly lit hall that was painted an institutional green and had soiled brown carpeting covering the floor. When I came to another door I waited, knowing that cameras were watching me. With a click, the door unlocked and I walked inside.

Another world greeted me. Phones rang, printers clattered, and rows of computer terminals staffed with people intent on their duties were busy doing their jobs. It was 1995 and the agency had all the latest technology.

The young man at the desk just inside the door looked up from his terminal. He had a crewcut and the identification badge hanging around his neck read *David*.

"Kathryn Austin. I have a two o'clock appointment."

David examined his clipboard. "Room one, down the hall and to the left," he said, before turning his back on me and returning to his terminal.

I had never been in room one. My previous assignments took place in rooms with a higher number, usually eight or ten. I unbuttoned my coat, slipped it off, and put it over my arm with an uneasy feeling that something was going to be different about this assignment.

"Intervene," the International Intervention Agency, was an obscure, little known office of the government. They dealt with unusual cases of theft, fraud, extortion, terrorism, or anything else that had international connections. I never really knew exactly how they operated beyond my limited, short-term assignments with them. A month earlier I had worked alongside more experienced agents on a team to capture a group of Russians selling imitation Coach Bags. I called it the "Coach Bag Caper."

†

I knocked on the door, entered the room, looked around, and took a deep breath knowing this was not going to be a routine assignment. Seated to the left behind a large, polished, walnut desk was my contact at the agency, Michele, dressed as usual in a stylish, tailored, navy-blue suit. She had her dark brown hair pulled back and was wearing horn-rimmed glasses. I thought of this as her no-nonsense look. Seated next to her behind the desk, and obviously in command, was another woman. Michele motioned to a chair. I sat down.

"How are you today, Kathryn?" The artificial expression on Michele's face suggested a smile.

"I'm fine, thank you."

5

They both looked down to open folders in front of them and I waited in the silence that followed. If they were trying to intimidate me they were succeeding. As the woman I did not know examined her folder, I studied her. She was older, perhaps early sixties, tall, a short sensible hairstyle, thick bifocals, and a simple but expensive suit. I had never seen her before, but I had my suspicions.

Michele arranged her papers before looking up. "This is our Chief of Operations, Dr. Caldwell."

"How do you do, Dr. Caldwell?" She nodded curtly in my direction.

"Do you like opera?" Michele asked brightly.

"Yes, somewhat. I guess I'm more involved with instrumental music." I added, "You know I play with a recorder group." Why did they suddenly care about my musical interests?

"You have the option of declining this assignment if you wish to." Michele looked down at the papers in front of her. Her earlier expression meant to suggest a smile had disappeared.

I waited in silence until Michele continued. "We are concerned about a terrorist group that has been silent for several years, and we were under the impression they had disbanded. Several recent incidents lead us to believe they are still active, and an opera singer who possibly is their leader is linked to them."

Michele turned over some pages of her folder. "They are known as the White Moon. They had a mixed political agenda that started with the Vietnam War. Then other causes came along. We think they are now networking in Europe with other terrorist groups. They have been responsible for bombings in areas with easy public access such as subways and crowded streets." She turned another page. "There was an incident in London ten months ago, coincidentally at the time this woman was appearing there in an opera. We didn't immediately suspect her, but one of the White Moon members apprehended after the London bombing claimed during interrogation that the leader was a woman, well-known in the opera world and currently in London. This description covered several singers and also a stage designer. Before the White Moon member could be questioned further she committed suicide in her cell."

Dr. Caldwell tapped a finger on some papers in her file and adjusted her glasses. "Since that time, by various means, we believe we have eliminated every suspect except one woman."

Michele withdrew a photograph from her folder, placed it on the desk facing me, and sat back in her chair, her eyes never leaving me.

I picked up a glamorous publicity photo of an attractive woman in an elaborate gown, her dark hair swept up, and wearing a heavy, jeweled necklace. She was evidently in costume for an operatic role. Her pose was sensual and yet her expression was innocent.

"Adriana Desi. We would like to know who her friends are, whom she meets and whom she calls. Everything you can find out about her." Michele continued watching me.

I was puzzled because surveillance was not my area of expertise. "You want me to follow her?"

Dr. Caldwell and Michele exchanged a brief glance. Dr. Caldwell leaned forward in her chair and looked at me. "We want you to meet her, get to know her. Become intimate if necessary."

I could feel myself blushing. Had I heard her right?

Michele reached over and took the photograph from me. "Before we go any further, we know you are not currently romantically involved with anyone and expect you to stay that way during this assignment. Is that understood?"

"Yes." I nodded, resigned to the fact that nothing in my life was private.

There was a pause and I assumed that they accepted my answer since Michele said, "We have biographical information for you to read and a list of places in the city that she is known to frequent. Also, we are including more background on the White Moon."

"I'm afraid I don't understand why she is going to want to meet me. What do we have in common that would be of interest to her?" I asked in some confusion.

Michele withdrew another photograph from the folder and handed it to me. The compression of the street scene told me a long lens had taken it. I stared in disbelief. Everyone has a twin somewhere so they say and there, walking next to Adriana Desi, was another woman. "Do you see a resemblance?"

I looked up to see them both watching me and I detected a faint smile on Dr. Caldwell's face. "Yes," I faltered for a moment, "the other woman looks like me."

"Nicole Chapman, companion and lover of Adriana Desi."

I thought I must be really slow today and shook my head. "But, if she has her, why would she want to meet me?"

Michele responded. "Nicole is dead…killed in a car accident seven months ago. Adriana was so devastated that she canceled all her appearances and has not performed since."

I looked at the picture again. There was something in the other woman's face. It was an intensity that I did not have. I put the picture down.

Michele picked up the photograph. "We know Nicole was a member of the White Moon and living on a farm upstate. After her death we located it but they had all fled, leaving behind some starving cats and dogs. We suspect that Adriana recruited Nicole Chapman into the White Moon. We want to know who the other members are, who else she might have recruited, what their plans are, and anything else you can learn about them."

Dr. Caldwell picked up her folder and held it out to me. "Read this over and study it. Michele will give you a room to work in. Have some coffee, take your time. You will be reporting to Michele directly." Focusing her penetrating gaze on me she added, "Kathryn, we are depending on you."

I took the folder. They didn't ask if I wanted to refuse the assignment. By accepting the folder I was accepting the assignment.

Michele stood to lead me to my room. "Don't worry about work. Ask for vacation days, as you need them. I'm sure they will understand."

My assignments with the agency were sporadic and short-term. My real job was working as a chemist at a drug-testing laboratory. When I returned from my tour with the Peace Corps, the lab had contacted me, offering me a job. I assumed it was because I was on a list of returned volunteers looking for work and had a graduate chemistry degree and laboratory experience. Shortly after that the agency had approached me. Looking back, I wondered if they worked together. Using my generous vacation days, I always had time off for the assignments and the pay was unusually good.

Dr. Caldwell stood, nodded at me, and left the room, effectively dismissing me.

†

Michele and I walked silently down the hall to my room. I wondered if she was uneasy with my assignment, but the agency knew my background and lifestyle. I suspected they had probably asked others to do more.

As I sat at a table in the room with a cup of coffee and my folder of information, Michele pointed to my long blond hair. "Get your hair cut, not too much, just shoulder length." She said nothing more, turned and left the room.

I read through the folder trying to memorize details about a woman I doubted I would be able to meet, much less gain any information from. When I finally picked up my cup the coffee was cold and I had gone through the folder three times. Chilled, exhausted, and overwhelmed by my assignment, I closed the folder.

†

Out in the parking lot my former joyful mood was gone. Dark gray clouds now covered the sky, the temperature had dropped, and the sun was setting. This time of year darkness came early and it reflected my mood. Hugging my coat around me I walked across the lot to my car. This was my only extravagance, a British racing green 1972 MGB, used only in decent weather on my occasional days off or on the weekends. I unlocked the door, got in, and started the engine.

It was rush hour and my plans for the afternoon had included a trip to the museum to see a new exhibit of Ming dynasty pottery and do some shopping, but those plans were now forgotten. The descriptions of the terrible acts of the White Moon contrasting with the glamorous photos of the opera singer crowded my mind. I pushed them aside to concentrate on getting home to the warmth of my small apartment.

Chapter Two

Saturday I worked at the lab, and with the Christmas holiday approaching, the workload had slowed and the hours dragged, making the day seem endless.

At my lunch break in the employee lounge, I always tried to get a table in the corner away from the loud conversations of my co-workers. Today they were complaining about ungrateful husbands as I sat alone eating a cheese sandwich while huddled over an Agatha Christie mystery. Thoughts of my unwanted agency assignment crowded my mind and, as a distraction, my eyes wandered to the others in the room.

Dawn, a clerk in the front office, pulled a thick salami sandwich out of her lunch bag, rustling the waxed paper as she unwrapped it. "I told Bob it's about time he picked up after himself around the house. I have enough to do." She tossed back her long brown hair and looked around the room to nodding heads. I averted my eyes as she took a large bite out of the bulging sandwich.

I sniffed the air, realizing that bringing leftovers for lunch must be popular since the whole room smelled of meatloaf mingled with some spicy Italian dish.

LuAnn, a chemist, had finished her lunch and now reached in and pulled a magazine from a large tote bag she had recently begun carrying around with her. The bag had a pattern of teddy bears on it, all performing some cute act such as playing a drum, waving a flag, or throwing a football. Thin and pale, with a new tight perm, she never had much to say during the group conversations at lunch. Now, she listened to the husband complaints, occasionally nodding her agreement, but not offering anything.

Although two of the lab technicians joined in sharing grievances about their families, I knew none of them would ever consider any other life.

The lunch break ended, I returned to my analyzer, working until finally the day was over. I hurried home to my apartment in the growing darkness. Perhaps it was because of having to listen to family talk all day that I decided to go to the bar that night.

As I stood in the hot shower and ran a soapy hand down my left leg I thought about my assignment. The background information described how the White Moon members had a tattoo of a crescent moon on their upper left thigh. I looked down at my left leg and wondered how it would look with the tattoo. Which way did the moon face? How big was it?

†

In Greenwich Village it was still early for the bar scene and I easily found a parking place on the street. It had been several months since I had been to Ruby's, my favorite women's bar, and I tried to appear nonchalant and blend in behind a group who were all laughing and talking together. I remembered the times I came here with my friends, all laughing as these were now.

In the dim lighting, I tried to decide where to sit. Some areas of the long U-shaped bar were the unofficial property of groups of women who resented others sitting there. Recalling an incident one night when a woman had belligerently told another to move to a different spot, I chose what I thought would be a neutral area near a post. Everything was the same, the pictures of favorite lesbian movie stars, singers, and athletes hung on the walls. There was the pool table in the back room and the jukebox playing 'Look Away' by Chicago. Upstairs was a dance floor, but as I settled on a stool at the bar, I knew that tonight I wasn't in the mood to go up there. Despite the familiar atmosphere of Ruby's I felt awkward being there alone.

I didn't recognize the bartender, a tall young girl with curly red hair, freckles, and a friendly manner. She slapped a coaster on the bar and gave me a broad smile. "Hi. What can I get you?"

"I think I'll have a Heineken." I preferred a glass of wine, but a beer would be easier to linger over.

She brought the beer and I noticed her carefully wiping a spot on the already clean bar. "Wonder if we'll have snow for Christmas," she said.

The weather was always a safe subject. I smiled and rose to the occasion. "I don't know. It's probably too early to tell."

"Talk to you later." I watched her move down the bar to take care of two new arrivals.

I sipped my beer and discreetly glanced around. No one looked familiar. It was early yet and I knew that by eleven the place would be full. I didn't plan on staying that long. After some small talk with a few women near me, I relaxed and sipped my beer watching all these women enjoying each other's company wondering why I had waited so long to come back.

I was reaching for my money on the bar when a hand touched my shoulder. "Kat, how are you?" My heart was pounding as she sat on the stool next to me. I had been prepared to be calm and detached when the day came that we met again.

Kitty James signaled the bartender, ordered a beer, and pointed to my glass. "Give her one, too." Kitty turned to look at me. "You look pretty good. Maybe you've lost a little weight, not that you needed to. Your hair is shorter." She smiled. "I like it."

Following Michele's orders, I had had my hair trimmed to shoulder length. I had to admit afterwards that it looked good, and now I was doubly glad I did it. "You're looking great, too." I couldn't think of anything else to say and it was the truth.

"Unlike you, I've put on some weight." She sighed. "I've got to get back to my routine. It was pretty hectic this summer, and I didn't have much time to run or work out."

When we were together, Kitty and I always found the time to run, swim, and work out. She was taller than I, and I remembered her athletic body. Now in a ski jacket, I couldn't tell if she was heavier or not. She did have the same long, dark hair and lively, warm, brown eyes.

15

"How's life at the urine factory?" Kitty grinned at me over her glass.

Since the lab specialized in drug testing, and most of our specimens were urine samples, this had been her name for the place. "It's the same." I had to ask, "Are you still with the doctor?" I knew her name was really Dr. Mary Beth Neuhausen, up and coming pathologist, but there was no way I was going to let Kitty know that I remembered that.

"Yes." Kitty sipped her beer and looked across the room.

"Are you living with her?" I don't know why I asked since it was none of my business anymore.

"Well, I'm staying at her place for a few days. She's in Chicago at a seminar presenting a paper. I'm watching her cats."

I suspected the doctor would not jeopardize her career by openly living with another woman.

"Everything's fine. She's pretty busy with long hours at the hospital and meetings all the time. In January, she takes over as Chief of Staff. You know she has an image to be careful about." I thought Kitty was attempting to sound overly enthusiastic about her relationship with the doctor and with having to be discreet about the relationship. It was so unlike Kitty.

Kitty and I had lived together until Dr. Neuhausen decided she had to become computer literate. Kitty, a systems analyst who taught computer classes on the side, took the job to bring the doctor up to speed.

Kitty had always been so independent and sure of herself and that was what attracted me to her in the first place. No doubt it attracted the doctor also. I remember when I met her.

I was in a trendy new place called Café Lulu to meet some members of my recorder group. I was so surprised to see Kitty, sitting at a table with a woman I didn't recognize. When I passed by her, I couldn't pretend I didn't know her. I stopped abruptly and Kitty introduced me. "Kathryn, this is Dr. Mary Beth Neuhausen." She turned to the woman. "Kathryn was one of my computer students."

Upset at Kitty's lie about our relationship, I stared at the slim, cool, and intelligent-looking woman who was dressed in an expensive but conservative suit. She extended her hand for a weak handshake and turned back to Kitty. I mumbled something about being pleased to meet her and hurried away, feeling betrayed by Kitty.

"So, what have you been doing besides working?" Kitty shifted to face me.

"Not much really." She had never known the exact nature of my occasional work for the agency. I always let her assume that it was a research project involving returned Peace Corps volunteers. It was only in the last year since she left me that I had taken on more frequent assignments.

"Are you with someone now?" Kitty asked in a casual tone.

"No, I'm not." My private life was no business of hers.

Kitty took a sip of her beer. "I'm surprised. I thought you would be by now." She smiled and motioned with her eyes. "That woman over there looks interested," she added. "And I've seen several others in here checking you out."

I looked up to see a slim woman with short black hair trying to make eye contact with me. "I'm not interested. I don't want anyone." I picked up my beer and took a small sip, looking in the other direction.

Kitty ran her fingers down the glass. "I've thought about you so often. I'm sorry it ended the way it did."

Kitty had moved out just before last Christmas when the doctor demanded her all for herself. I knew from her comments that Kitty was impressed with her money and position of power at the hospital, things I didn't feel I could compete with. At first, I had been in denial—Kitty wouldn't do that to me. Then I was angry with her, and finally, I accepted the fact that she had left me and was not coming back. I was about to answer her when a voice from behind stopped me.

"Are you two together?" Startled, we turned around. A short woman with orange-blonde hair piled on her head stood behind us. Her T-shirt, stretched over large breasts, had a simulated nametag that read 'Princess.'

Kitty finished her beer. "Why do you ask?"

"I thought maybe you'd like to go upstairs and dance." She turned a flirtatious look on Kitty.

"No, I'm with someone."

She turned to me. "How about you?"

"I'm not interested," I said, resenting her interrupting us. Shrugging she walked away.

We watched her leave.

"Pest," Kitty said. "Look, let's get out of here and go to my place. We could have some decent wine and talk. I already fed the cats so they can wait until morning."

For the past year, I had imagined the moment when Kitty and I would be together again. But tonight she was lonely, and tomorrow night when the doctor returned, she'd forget me. "Thanks, but I don't think it's a good idea. I better go." I fumbled with my change. "Bye, Kitty," I said before sliding off the stool

"Take care of yourself, Kat."

At the door, I turned to see Kitty watching me leave.

✝

That night as I lay in bed, I thought about Kitty calling me "Kat." Her first name was Katherine, and when we first met she began calling me Kat. She thought it was cute that we were Kitty and Kat. No one else had ever called me that and no one did now. After meeting her tonight, I wondered if the loneliness and unhappiness was finally leaving and I was starting to feel free again. It had taken almost a year.

Chapter Three

Friday morning in the lab, I was in the middle of performing the weekly maintenance on one of our analyzers. Dr. Amy Lan's trim figure came hurrying through the lab in her usual brisk manner, her white lab coat flying behind her, and looking up, I saw she had stopped and was standing next to me.

"Kathryn, when you are finished with the maintenance here, could I see you in my office?"

I glanced at the timer. "Yes, I have about ten minutes more."

"Fine." She turned abruptly and left the lab area for her office.

Now what could this be about? I wasn't in any trouble. Was I?

I found it difficult to concentrate on what I was doing as I reviewed Dr. Lan's request. Her tone was cold, but then it always was. Done with my maintenance, and after taking off my lab coat and washing my hands, I hurried out of the lab to Dr. Lan's office.

†

Dr. Lan's office door was open but I knocked on the doorway. "Come in, and please close the door." Her face was expressionless as she motioned toward a chair.

I sat on the edge of the chair and waited while Dr. Lan marked her place in a large procedure manual, and then closed it with a thump. Like Michele at the agency, Dr. Lan was a private person. I guessed she was about the same age as Michele, but her black hair had a few steaks of gray, giving her a striking appearance. She looked at me thoughtfully with her dark almond eyes, while I shifted uncomfortably in my chair.

"Kathryn, I need your help with something."

"Oh, are we setting up a new procedure?" This was something I always enjoyed.

She pursed her lips, and pushed the manual aside. "No, nothing like that. I feel I can trust you, and I'm not sure what to do about this situation."

Completely baffled by what she needed from me, I waited. Whatever it was, I could tell by the look on her face and her whole demeanor that it wasn't good.

"Someone has been stealing from the lab."

"Stealing from the lab?" I sounded like a parrot.

"This has been going on for over a month. The first week in November, we received six columns for the HPLC analyzer. A week later, when I did an inventory, they were all gone. None had been put into use. Luckily I caught this before we had to change a column. Three weeks ago, a

21

carton of Triage drug testing kits disappeared. The log shows they were never used." She sighed. "Yesterday I checked in a new electronic pipettor, still in the box; it is gone. There've been other incidents that I documented after the columns disappeared."

This problem seemed to be beyond me but I wanted to help Dr. Lan. I had a great deal of respect for her as a scientist and for the way she ran the lab. As I sat there, a thought occurred to me. "One idea I would suggest is to look at who has been hired since these thefts began."

She nodded. "Yes, that's a good suggestion. If you see anything suspicious, or have any further ideas, I would appreciate it."

I stood. "I'll keep my eyes open." As soon as I said it, I realized it was a trite remark, and added lamely, "Maybe I can think of something else."

Dr. Lan frowned and looked up at me. "I've never had to deal with anything like this." For a moment I sensed a vulnerability that I had never seen in her. Then she opened the manual on her desk and looked down at it. "Thank you, Kathryn. You may leave the door open."

As I walked back to the lab I realized that this was the most personal conversation I had ever had with Dr. Lan. In the past, we had worked together on implementing procedures and setting up new analyzers, but these were always technical, business-only collaborations. I had no idea what Dr. Lan did outside the lab. Her sparsely furnished office did not contain the usual pictures of children and a husband. Not even a pet's picture. I never knew her to socialize outside work when some of the lab employees stopped for a drink on a special occasion. But then, I never did either.

I returned to my analyzer and began performing the tests for the day, but now I looked around at all my co-workers with suspicion, wondering if any of them were responsible for the thefts. Then again, it could be someone else, like maintenance or cleaning workers. I didn't like feeling this way and wished I hadn't become involved.

Chapter Four

Sunday morning I got up early and pulled on my running clothes to go out for a short run and buy the paper. The weather was cool, crisp, and sunny, with only a slight breeze rustling the bare tree branches. I ran longer than usual, enjoying the freedom of a day off work and being outdoors.

After a leisurely breakfast with the paper, I decided it was time to do some research for my unwanted agency assignment. That meant going back outside where the weather had changed and was rapidly becoming overcast and windy. While walking to the library, I pulled my collar up around my neck as I mentally reviewed what I knew about my assignment. I couldn't see how I would ever manage to meet Adriana Desi. If I did, what would she be like? She was a famous opera star, and I could imagine her as demanding, imperiously issuing orders to all those around her. Maybe, in true diva fashion, she would have a fiery temper, scream, and throw things if she didn't have her way. With her glamorous lifestyle, how could she ever be interested in me? Perhaps she already had a new lover. The only possibility was that she might consider me a promising recruit for the White Moon. But I even doubted that.

Before the library, I stopped at a large music store and, browsing in the operatic "D" section, found a recording entitled *Verdi Rarities* by Adriana Desi. The cover photo fascinated me. In the picture, she was wearing a simple, black, off-the-shoulder gown showing a hint of cleavage. Her dark hair was down around her shoulders and her expression was more thoughtful than dramatic or coy. I looked at the date—four years ago.

At the checkout counter the clerk, a tall young man with bleached blond hair, dramatically held up the recording and turned it over. "One of my favorites. She had a truly beautiful voice. This is a wonderful recording. She is on some others which we don't have in stock right now." He rang up the sale and took my money. "Such a shame about her vocal crisis, but I heard she will return to the Met this spring." He sighed dramatically. "We all hope she does."

When I reached the library and went inside, I was happy to be out of the cold chilly air. In the Periodicals Section of the library, I found a table, sat down, got out a pen and notebook, and began reading through back issues of *Opera News* magazine.

The background information at the agency had been concerned with the facts of her life. Born in Trieste in 1956, she was thirty-nine years old. After studying in Italy, she had sung in various small opera houses in Europe until her U.S. debut at Lyric Opera of Chicago, when she stepped in on opening night for an ailing singer in *Tosca*. After a tremendous reception by the audience and critics, the Met engaged her, and she had sung there every season since. Her beloved mother, who had devoted herself to the career of her only child, had always lived with her until her death two years earlier. She now resided in Manhattan.

The *Opera News* articles consisted of interviews and reviews of her roles over the years, praising her sumptuous tonal beauty, intelligent musicianship, stage presence, and devotion to "her art." A small article mentioned Desi canceling her performances in May because of illness, the impression given that her heavy schedule had caused extreme fatigue, and she was resting and expected to return in April.

Immersed in my reading and note taking, I had forgotten the time. Stretching my stiff legs, I looked across the room and out the window to see it was already growing dark. I gathered my notes and the articles I had copied, put on my coat, and prepared myself for departure. I knew nothing was waiting for me outside in the cold darkness.

†

On my way home, I stopped at Yen Chen, a Chinese restaurant in my neighborhood. While I waited for my takeout order, I had a glass of Wan Fu at the tiny bar. As I sipped my wine, I looked around at the familiar framed pictures of pandas and bamboo, the Chinese figurines in a glass case, and the red lanterns hanging from the ceiling among the red and gilt décor. In the past, Kitty and I had come here often. I didn't expect to see her now—the doctor wouldn't patronize this kind of place. The owner appeared from the kitchen with my bag of food and carefully set it down in front of me. I remembered how, in the past, he used to stop at our table and politely inquire if everything was all right.

"Your friend. I have not seen her, a long time."

"She," I hesitated, "she moved away."

He nodded. "Yes, I understand. Thank you."

I picked up my bag and left.

†

That evening after I ate my Chinese food I poured a glass of wine, went into the living room and sank into my comfortable tan corduroy chair, thinking about my life this past year. After Kitty left me, I had gradually moved away from our circle of friends. They were mostly couples, and at first, they had tried to introduce me to someone else who was alone, but I wasn't interested in any of the women. Soon it started to become awkward for me, so I eventually stopped frequenting the bars and returning their phone calls.

Not yet ready to go to bed, I picked up the recording I had bought on my way to the library that afternoon. The liner notes described Adriana Desi's voice as lush, fabulously warm with incredible control of volume, superb ability to phrase, and flawless lyricism.

In the darkness that night, I listened to a beautiful voice and fell in love with it.

Chapter Five

The next week I knew that, unless I attempted to meet Adriana Desi, the agency would be more displeased with me than usual. Thursday was my day off from the lab. Giving up my planned trip to the museum I headed for a restaurant where, according to my briefing notes, she often had lunch.

I entered the small Mediterranean restaurant, Bella, and quickly scanned all the tables in the back of the room. Seeing she was not there, I found a place at the crowded marble-topped bar where I could keep an eye on the entrance. Glancing over the drink menu, I ordered a glass of the least expensive white wine from the bartender, a middle-aged woman in a black shirt and striped vest with a red bow tie. As I sipped the wine, I busied myself looking over a recorder workshop brochure I had recently received in the mail. Reading the brochure reminded me that my quartet was rehearsing Saturday morning. Our schedule had us playing a

Christmas concert at a nursing home on Sunday. Since we had not rehearsed together for several weeks, I was apprehensive about the concert. I stuffed the brochure back in my purse and lingered over the glass of wine. When my glass was empty, the bartender approached me.

"Care for another glass of wine?" She picked up my glass and waited for my answer.

As if I had an urgent appointment, I examined my watch. "No thank you, I have to get going." The lunch hour was over, the restaurant was no longer busy, and I didn't think Adriana Desi was going to show up today. As I left the restaurant I wondered what I would have done if she had been there having lunch with friends. How would I approach her? I had no idea.

My next stop was Defoe's, a bookstore she liked to visit on her free afternoons. The large store was not one of the new superstores, but an independent with tall shelves that lined the walls and formed aisles, and created little areas where chairs were placed. Framed autographed photographs of authors who had visited the store over the years, some yellowing with age, covered every available remaining wall space. Tables in the center of the room held new releases, and magazines were in racks along a wall near the front of the store.

Taking my time, I covered the store, browsing in all the aisles and out of the way corners, looking for Adriana Desi. She was not in the store.

✝

On a cold, gloomy Saturday morning, my recorder group met at Joanna's home. The brownstone was located in a quiet neighborhood and had a spacious living room to accommodate our four chairs and music stands. Joanna had recently retired from her position as a college French professor, but seemed busier than ever. She also played clarinet with several amateur orchestras and a dance band, along with playing some obscure instrument in an early music ensemble. Playing with so many groups left her little time to practice her recorder, and it often showed during our rehearsals. She and I played alto while Eileen, an accountant with a small manufacturing firm, played the soprano.

Across from me, I watched Chris carefully putting her tenor together. Shorter than I, with a trim figure, she had a daringly short haircut. Chris was my favorite in the group or perhaps we just had more in common because I knew she lived with another woman. When the woman attended one of our performances, others who knew them had referred to "their place." I remembered the woman as short and plump with reddish-blond hair and a jovial manner. Often Chris and I would linger after a rehearsal so we could leave together and talk on the way to our cars. As a high school music teacher, Chris was the leader of our group and we deferred to her on musical decisions.

Two years ago, our group consisted of eight members, but other commitments, moving away, and health problems had taken their toll, so we were now down to what I thought of as the dysfunctional four.

Joanna put on her glasses, patted her graying hair, and arranged the music on her stand. "I have two other Christmas concerts coming up with my clarinet, not much time for my recorder lately." She shuffled through the music on her stand. "Let's see, what were we working on?"

Eileen pulled the music from her briefcase, grumbling. "You knew we had this concert scheduled. We all have a responsibility to be prepared." I noticed Eileen had a new perm, which gave her brown hair the appearance of a washboard. She scowled at the music as she placed it on her stand. "I would hope you've all been practicing this music."

Joanna didn't respond and Chris tactfully suggested we begin tuning. This was something we could all agree upon.

The rehearsal ended at noon, our program decided except for one piece.

"This Bach arrangement is too difficult. We have to delete it." Eileen picked the music off her stand and waved it emphatically.

"Such a shame." Joanna reluctantly set it aside. "It's so lovely."

"Well, we can't do it without more rehearsal time," Eileen snapped, while packing up her recorder and music.

"Maybe we can work on it for our next concert," I offered, hoping to avoid further disagreement. Chris sat silently and I sensed she was trying to ignore the whole exchange.

Eileen had seemed to be in a bad mood today, challenging some of the tempos and everyone's intonation. I decided it was holiday stress. The upcoming Christmas holiday with all its hype was a stressful time for many. People alone, as I was, dreaded it as a family time, while many of my co-workers complained that both sets of in-laws expected the holiday to be spent with them.

Chris sat swabbing out her recorder. "How's everything at the lab, Kathryn?"

"Slowing down, you know, with the holidays coming up." Before I could say anything further, Eileen made a face as she slammed her case shut.

"Must be nice. We're busier than ever. Everybody takes vacation and the rest of us are left with all the work."

31

"Well, I'm glad I have Christmas break coming up." Chris grinned at me.

Joanna laid her recorder aside. "I'm so glad I'm retired, none of that trouble anymore." She sighed. "But speaking of trouble, we had an unpleasant situation in my early wind group."

She paused and we all waited for the story to unfold.

"Joyce, who played in our group, owned this set of shawms, in all the voices."

Eileen put up her hand. "Wait a minute. What's a shawm?" She demanded.

Momentarily flustered at the interruption, Joanna paused and then went on. "Oh, it's a double reed medieval woodwind instrument, the predecessor of the modern oboe." She continued the story. "Well, two years ago, Joyce moved to North Carolina and left the shawms behind with our group. They needed work so we had them repaired and revoiced, but a few months ago, she wrote that she wanted her shawms. We were under the impression that she gave them to us, but her understanding was that she lent them to us until she was settled in her new home."

"Well, what happened?" Eileen asked impatiently

"In the end we kept them but paid her something for them. After all, we spent the money to repair them."

"Didn't you have anything in writing?" Chris fit the pieces of her recorder in the case and stuffed her music in a briefcase. "If you didn't, you should have."

Joanna shook her head. "No, unfortunately it was the end of a friendship between Joyce and most members of the group."

Eileen, who was ready to leave, started toward the door and turned back. "You're lucky she didn't sue you.

Those things must have been expensive." She left with a bang of the door.

I stifled a yawn. All this over a bunch of shawms.

Chris stood, slung her briefcase over her shoulder, and zipped her jacket. "Are you ready, Kathryn?"

I quickly packed up and pulled on my coat. "All set."

Chris and I left together and, as we walked down the front steps, she shifted her recorder case in her hands and looked at me sideways.

"Do you have any plans for after our concert tomorrow?"

"No, I don't have anything on."

"I thought maybe you would like to go get something to eat, have a drink."

"That would be great. I'll plan on it." I got in my car and drove away. I was already looking forward to meeting Chris after the concert. I wasn't sure why, I didn't want a relationship with her. Maybe I was just lonely with the Christmas season approaching and I would enjoy her company.

✝

That evening I retrieved a box from the back of the closet. Inside was a small tabletop Christmas tree. Last year after Kitty left me, I had not planned on having a tree, but a few days before Christmas, I saw it in a store and, on an impulse, bought it.

Removing a pile of books and magazines from the table in my living room, I placed the tree on it before finding an extension cord and plugging it in. The tiny white lights still worked, and with the red ornaments it looked quite festive, adding a little Christmas cheer to my apartment. I decided having the tree was just what I needed again this year and was determined not to feel sorry for myself any longer—last Christmas was behind me.

Chapter Six

Sunday afternoon, we four recorder players met for our concert in the recreation room of the nursing home. Overheated and with that distinctive smell that I couldn't define, it recalled all the depressing memories of visits to my aunt. Pushing them aside, I tried to concentrate on today's concert.

In deference to the upcoming holiday, our attire consisted of black slacks and a red top. Joanna wore a short, red-velvet jacket, while Chris and I both had on red sweaters, and Eileen sported a red-satin blouse. We set up our music stands, arranged our music, warmed up, and tuned, while we waited for the residents to drift in. The majority were women and some walked, others shuffled behind walkers, while aides pushed a few in wheelchairs.

When the residents were in place, the Activity Director, Liz, stepped up to a microphone. After a squeal of feedback, which brought a loud complaint from a resident, she introduced us. "We are so lucky to have a group of—" she consulted her notes, "players of the recorder, an ancient instrument I understand, who are going to play some lovely music for us." She smiled nervously, waved in our direction, and then moved over to watch from the side of the room.

I hoped the playing of lovely music was going to be true as we launched into the program with our Christmas medley. We ended the program to scattered applause and I thought the performance had gone fairly well. Joanna missed an entrance once, but caught up later. It was the kind of mistake only we would notice.

As soon as the concert ended, Eileen quickly packed up, mumbled holiday greetings to us, and left. Joanna took longer to put her recorder, stand, and music away, chatting all the time about an upcoming concert with her dance band. "I have to get going. Have a nice Christmas." She waved to Chris and me as she hurried away, nodding to residents as she passed them.

"See you at the bar," Chris said before leaving.

I stayed behind a few minutes talking with some of the residents, glad to hear that they enjoyed the music as they told me about the instruments they had played in their youth. When I was leaving, my thoughts were of my aunt when she lived in her nursing home amidst confusion and unhappiness.

I was an only child, and I had just graduated from college when my parents were killed in a car accident. They were driving home at night in the rain from a vacation in Door County, Wisconsin. Witnesses said my father skidded off the road when he pulled onto the shoulder to avoid an oncoming truck that was too close to his lane.

Six months before the accident, my mother had reluctantly moved my Aunt Emma, her older sister and only sibling, from the family home where she had lived all her life, to a nursing home because she could no longer take care of herself. I tried to explain the accident to my aunt, but although she attended the funeral, she continued to ask for her little sister.

Throughout all this, I depended on my lover, Jackie, an aspiring chef, for comfort and support. After almost a year together, she accused me of not being sufficiently committed to our relationship and left me. Devastated, I found out that two weeks later she took off to ski in Colorado with a woman she met in a bar. So much for her commitment.

Alone and unsure of what to do with my life, and with my substantial inheritance, I spent two years in graduate school and then joined the Peace Corps, hoping it would be a chance to get away and possibly do something to help someone else. A year earlier, my Aunt Emma had suffered a stroke and no longer knew me. I kept up the hope that on one of my visits she somehow might recognize me.

✝

I planned to meet Chris at a place she suggested. Chris, a beer drinker, boasted that this bar, Old Heidelberg, was one of her favorites and carried at least one hundred different brands from all over the world.

The weather had turned colder with dark clouds filling the sky as a few snowflakes drifted down and melted on my face and coat. Inside the warm, dark bar I saw heavy, wooden, ceiling beams, stained-glass windows, ornate steins, and a lot of German style décor including an impressive suit of armor.

Chris waved to me from a booth across the room and I walked quickly toward her. I took off my coat and slid in opposite her. "It's starting to snow. Maybe we'll have some for Christmas." I brushed some moisture from my hair.

The waitress, wearing what appeared to be a German folk outfit, came to take our order and waited while Chris examined the extensive beer list. She finally chose something foreign and exotic sounding, and I ordered a bottle of Heineken. When the waitress arrived with our bottles of beer I asked for a glass. She returned and plunked a heavy frosted glass mug on the table in front of me.

Chris took a drink, set down her bottle, and leaned back in the booth, running a hand through her short hair. "So, what are your Christmas plans?"

"I'm not sure yet." I was embarrassed to admit I had no idea what I would do.

"I'm going to Iowa with Barb to visit her family. She's one of eight children, should be quite a gathering."

I assumed Barb was her partner. I wondered what she did, how they had met, how long they had been together, but didn't feel I knew Chris well enough to ask her a lot of personal questions. She didn't offer anything further.

"How's your friend? The one that came to all our concerts last year."

I gripped the handle of my mug. "I don't see her anymore."

"Oh." There was an awkward pause. "I didn't know or I wouldn't have asked." Chris fumbled with her bottle.

"It's all right. All in the past." To change the subject I decided to tell Chris about the trouble at work. "We have a problem in the lab. It seems someone is stealing parts and supplies."

Chris rolled her eyes. "No kidding. I guess that happens in a lot of work places. What's even worse is when they embezzle money. You know, writing checks on some phony account and keeping the money."

"Yes," I agreed. "That's pretty bad."

"What are they doing about it?"

"My supervisor is checking to see who has been hired since the thefts started."

Chris raised her bottle. "Sounds like a good idea. Hope you catch the person." She took a long drink and looked around for the waitress.

We ordered hamburgers and another beer. While we waited for the food, Chris nervously peeled the corner of the label on her beer bottle. "Kathryn, I'm not planning to continue with our recorder group." She looked up at me.

"But, Chris, it will be the end of the group." Shocked and disappointed, I hesitated. "We need you. Don't quit."

"I'm sorry but I can't stand playing with Joanna any longer. She drives me crazy with her poor intonation and sloppy playing. And Eileen is always in a bad mood. Besides, my high school orchestra is going to Europe this summer and I'll be busy with rehearsals. I just won't have time for the group."

Accurate as it may have been, I was uncomfortable with the criticism of Joanna's playing. Weren't we all amateurs, supposedly playing for our own enjoyment? As for Eileen, I too had had enough of her ill humor.

The hamburgers arrived and Chris spread catsup on hers. "Do you cross-country ski?"

"Yes, but I didn't do any last year." This was because Kitty left me before we had any snow and I never skied after that.

When Kitty and I were together, we skied every winter, and always spent a weekend at the Little Switzerland Ski Resort. I remembered skiing the trails in the morning and

39

having our lunch in an old building that had once been a barn. In the afternoon, we skied other trails and then ended up soaking in the whirlpool tub in our room at the resort. Before dinner, there were drinks in front of the roaring fire in the massive, fieldstone fireplace, and later dinner in the alpine-style dining room with its high-beamed ceiling, antler chandeliers, and rustic, carved, wooden furniture. At night, we made love in the huge bed under a thick down comforter.

I wondered if Kitty went there with the doctor now. I could easily picture the doctor in a smart expensive outfit, sitting in front of the fireplace, holding a glass of wine, or eating in the dining room. I could not picture her on the ski trails. With an effort, I pulled my attention back to Chris.

"A bunch of us go to this place where they have great trails, we stay at a nature center nearby," she said enthusiastically. "You bring your own sleeping bags and they have a place where you can cook your meals. If you'd like to join us, I'll let you know when we go. That is," she added, "if we have some good snow over a weekend."

It sounded a little primitive for me, but I supposed it might be fun.

We finished our meal and drinks, paid the check, and then went outside to stand on the sidewalk in front of the bar. Heavy snowflakes fell around us.

Chris turned up her jacket collar and shoved her hands in her pockets. "I'll call you about the skiing."

"I'd like that. You know I feel badly about you leaving the group. I wish you'd reconsider." Chris didn't reply and I didn't know what else to say to change her mind.

We parted. Chris turned and waved to me as she walked away, and I wondered if I would ever see her again.

Chapter Seven

Monday morning when I reported to the agency, Michele got out the folder of background information, sighed, and opened the cover. "Let's go over the places Desi is known to regularly visit. We really want to move ahead with this." She looked up. "Have you had enough time off work?"

I nodded. Trying to defend myself, I mumbled. "Yes, I just haven't been able to meet her yet." I knew if it were not for my striking resemblance to Nicole Chapman, they wouldn't have given me this important assignment.

"Kathryn, I suggest you make another visit, or as many as necessary, to these places until you find her." Michele tapped the folder with a finger and leaned back in her chair, dismissing me.

"Yes, I will." Despite my reassuring words, I felt this assignment was hopeless. What if I never managed to meet her?

I left the agency and was walking to my car when I heard someone calling my name. Turning, I saw a slim, attractive woman hurrying toward me. "Carmen!" I waited for her to catch up to me and we embraced.

"Kathryn, how are you? I didn't know you were at the agency today. I've wondered how you were doing."

I remembered when we first met...

Carmen and I met in September at the agency shooting range. Few women went there and as we walked out together, we began talking. This led to dinner at an Italian restaurant in the West Village. I learned that Carmen Manzano came to the U.S. from Puerto Rico, at the age of seven, with her mother and grandmother. I found her sparkling black eyes, long, wavy dark hair, and fine complexion attractive.

At dinner, she picked up her wine glass and leaned forward. "Kathryn, am I right, you like women?"

"Yes, Carmen, but I don't have anyone now and don't think I can handle a relationship." I briefly told her about my break up with Kitty.

Carmen frowned and nodded. "I understand. I loved someone. We had our differences, she was younger, and came from a family with money, but I thought she cared about me. When she was accepted at Stanford Law School, she took off for California and left me behind."

I already disliked the woman that I had never met. "So, she wanted to be a lawyer."

"Oh, I do too. I go to City University of New York Law School." Her face took on a determined look. "I'm going to specialize in Elder Law."

Our food arrived and Carmen continued her story. "After my mother died, I was brought up by my grandmother. Before she died there were many legal problems for her, and even though I couldn't help her then, perhaps I can help others."

We met once more in early November at the shooting range, and had a drink together afterward promising to stay in touch. This was the first time we had seen each other since then.

Now, standing in the parking lot next to my car, Carmen asked. "Are you on an assignment, Kathryn?" We were not allowed to discuss our current work with the other agents, but Carmen and I knew just how much information we could exchange without getting into trouble.

"I'm supposed to be trying to meet a woman whom the agency thinks is the head of a terrorist group."

I saw the concern in Carmen's eyes. "Kathryn, that sounds dangerous."

"Oh, I don't think so," I said airily. "The agency is wrong. She's not the type to do that kind of thing. And besides, I may never get to meet her."

"Well, be careful." Carmen poked at the ground with the toe of her stylish heel.

I waited for her to continue.

"I'm not happy with my meeting today. I don't feel comfortable about my assignment."

"Tell them you don't want it," I said.

"I can't. I need the money for school." Carmen's expression brightened. "Kathryn, let's get together before Christmas."

"Great. You can come to my place. I'm no cook, but we can have a pizza and beer."

"That would be fun, let me call you."

"Don't forget." We hugged goodbye, and as I watched Carmen walk away, I was looking forward to seeing her again.

After Carmen left, I thought about driving upstate to try to find the farm where the White Moon members had once lived. During my meeting with Michele and Dr. Caldwell, I had seen the address of the farm on a sheet in Michele's folder. I was proud of myself that I was able to read it upside down.

I discarded the idea when I considered it further. The agency would not appreciate me investigating something not assigned to me, and they had already located the farm, and found it abandoned. Still, it might have been interesting to see the place where Desi supposedly commanded the White Moon. Instead, I decided that I'd better make another effort to meet Adriana Desi since I was committed to this assignment, and Michele was not happy with my efforts so far. Not in the mood to sit alone over a glass of wine at the bar of the Mediterranean restaurant, I headed for the bookstore.

†

After driving around for fifteen minutes, I found a place on the street about a block from the bookstore. The sky was overcast, warmer than the day before, and it was not cold enough to snow. Instead, a light rain had begun to fall. I

44

always kept an umbrella behind the seat and, much as I disliked hauling it around, for some unknown reason I took it with me to the bookstore.

Inside, I briefly glanced around and then began to explore the store. I found it difficult to concentrate on looking for Adriana Desi. I loved books so much that I found myself stopping to examine the books in every section, and I lost track of my mission.

Just before I gave up my search for the day, I stopped at a table of big, glossy, gift books for the holiday season. As I was turning the pages of a book on the history of trains, I looked up to see a woman emerging from the aisle of the mystery section. Our eyes met and she stopped abruptly, dropping the books she was carrying. I stepped forward and picked up the books. She stood staring at me as I handed them to her.

"Thank you." She seemed to recover from what looked like the shock of seeing me, although her hands shook as she took the books from me.

"You're welcome." I nodded as she turned and hurried away. I returned to browsing through the books on the table, while watching for Adriana Desi to pay for her books and leave.

As soon as she left the store, I followed her. Gusts of wind blew sheets of rain and people huddled in doorways or under umbrellas. Opening my umbrella, I looked around. Adriana Desi was trying to get a taxi, signaling from under the cover of the bookstore awning. It was now nearing the busiest time of the day and no one stopped. I approached with my umbrella as she anxiously looked around, and our eyes met. She searched my face, obviously upset.

"It's hard to get a taxi here this time of day," I said.

"I know. I waited too long." She looked at her watch. "I have an appointment."

I stepped toward her with my umbrella. "Which direction are you going? I have a car."

She hesitated. "Lincoln Center, but certainly one of these will stop." She desperately signaled a taxi, which sped by throwing up tails of water behind it.

"I'm going that way. My car is right up the block." I extended the umbrella to include her.

She turned to me. "Thank you. That is kind of you."

We moved away and when we got to my car, I held it over her as I unlocked the door. She got in.

Inside the car, I was acutely aware of her presence, detecting the faint scent of her perfume. Unlike the glamorous publicity photos, she wore her dark hair simply pulled back and the minimum of makeup gave her a fresh, youthful appearance. As I busied myself starting the car and pulling into traffic, I could feel her looking at me.

"I have to apologize if I stared at you back in the bookstore." She hesitated. "It's… just that you so much resemble someone I knew and it startled me."

I noticed she had a slight accent, possibly Italian. "They say everyone has a twin." As soon as I said it, I thought what a stupid remark it was. I had finally met her, here we were together in my car, and now I couldn't think of anything intelligent to say.

"Isn't this weather unusual for December?" she asked. "I wonder if we will have snow for Christmas."

As she looked out the window, I glanced over at her attractive profile. Not wanting to run my car into anything, I quickly looked back to the traffic. "I don't know. I would guess we should have snow for Christmas." More bright conversation from me.

"I like this car. It must be fun in the summer with the top down. Is it old?"

"It's a 1972, in what they describe as mint condition."

"Lovely car." She ran her hand over the dashboard.

We were approaching Lincoln Center. "Do you want me to stop in front?"

"If you can, that would be fine." The rain had let up as I pulled over to the curb in front of the plaza. She turned to face me, putting out her hand. "I haven't introduced myself. Adriana Desi."

"Kathryn Austin." I took her hand and looked into her dark, expressive eyes, thinking that in person she was even lovelier than her photos.

"You don't know how much I appreciate this." She paused. "Kathryn, could I take you to lunch? If you give me your phone number, I'll call and we can pick a date."

Still at a loss for words I managed to say, "Yes, I could...would like that." I recited my number, unable to believe this was really happening.

She took a small appointment book and a pen from her purse. I watched a lock of her dark hair fall over her face as she held the book in her lap and carefully wrote my phone number in it.

Turning, I reached for the umbrella behind her seat. "Take this. It might be raining when you come out." I wanted it to pour so she couldn't leave my car.

"Oh, I can't. You'll need it."

"No, please take it. Everyone has trouble with the latch," I said, as I confidently reached across to open the door and then fumbled with it.

After she got out, I handed the umbrella to her along with her bag from the bookstore. She bent down and looked into my car, smiling at me. "Thank you again, Kathryn, I'll call you."

I watched her cross the plaza and pass the fountain, and after she disappeared inside I put the car in gear and drove away. Her scent still lingered in my car, and on the way home I tried to recall every detail of our meeting. The way she looked at me, the touch of her hand, and the sound of her voice. I even envisioned us flying down a country road together on a sunny day with the top down. Then I realized this was all part of my assignment, a contrived meeting. She would never know I was deceiving her. It was my job, and for the first time I was ashamed of what I had to do.

✝

That evening, as I was going through some old receipts, the phone rang. I eagerly reached for it, expecting it to be Carmen.

"Hello, Kathryn, this is Adriana Desi. How are you? I thought perhaps we could have lunch together if you have a free time."

I had been uncertain if I would ever hear from her. My mind raced ahead. I could get the time off work. "I'm free Wednesday if that is all right for you."

"That would be good. Would you like to meet me at Bella? Do you know it?"

It was the Mediterranean restaurant where I had been searching for her. "Yes, I've heard of it. What time is good for you? How is one o'clock?"

"That would be fine. See you then, Kathryn."

I hung up, unable to believe I was going to have lunch with Adriana Desi.

†

At the lab Tuesday morning, I approached Dr. Lan to ask for Wednesday off. "I have some important business to take care of."

She glanced at me briefly and then made a note on the schedule. "Yes, that will be all right."

Late Wednesday morning, I stopped at the agency on my way to the restaurant, expecting Michele to be pleased with my progress. Instead, she frowned and fingered some papers on her desk.

"Lunch? I would have preferred dinner. Lunchtime is hurried, evening would be more leisurely, a few drinks, relaxing, more time to talk and get acquainted." She impatiently pushed the papers aside. "Oh well, it's a start."

Disappointed at her reaction, I sat there waiting, but Michele had nothing more to say. As I stood to leave, she stopped me with a warning. "Kathryn, I want you to always remember when you are with her, this woman is dangerous."

I left the agency, walked to my car and started for the restaurant. What had I gotten myself into?

Chapter Eight

Arriving at Bella, I scanned the tables to see Adriana Desi sitting alone in the dining room. As I eagerly crossed the room toward her, she looked up and waved to me, but I had an eerie sensation that, from the delighted expression on her face, she was seeing me as Nicole Chapman.

"Hello Kathryn. I'm so glad you could meet me for lunch." She smiled warmly and I was Kathryn Austin now, not Nicole.

The waiter brought us water, handed us menus, took our order for a glass of wine, and left. She set her menu aside.

"I want to apologize. I hope I wasn't rude when I met you in the bookstore. I was so startled. You see, as I told you, there was someone I knew who looked so much like you."

"That is strange isn't it?" I shifted uncomfortably in my chair. What a fraud I was. How convenient of the agency to have me to use for this assignment. "I also must apologize. After you introduced yourself and I left you at the Lincoln Center, I realized that you were a very famous, wonderful opera singer. I should have recognized your name right away. I went out and got your recording of the *Verdi Rarities*. I enjoyed it so much that I have just about worn it out." At least this was true.

She sighed with pleasure. "Ah, making that recording was so enjoyable." She picked up her menu and looked down. "Perhaps you know I haven't performed for seven months."

"I think I read that somewhere," I mumbled.

Looking up she smiled shyly. "I will be appearing here at the Met in April, and there may be something before that." She shrugged. "We will see."

Again, I noticed her slight accent, which was charming and added an exotic element to her personality. Lifting my water glass, I looked at her over the rim. Wearing a light-weight, wool suit in a rose color complimented her dark hair and eyes. She looked lovelier than I remembered.

The wine arrived and she held up her glass. "To our new friendship."

We took a sip of our wine and she gazed across at me. "Kathryn, tell me about yourself. I don't know what you do, where you live."

"Nothing very interesting. I am a chemist at a lab that specializes in drug testing. We do medical and forensic testing for a variety of clients."

"Now that does sound interesting, I want to hear more about it." She put her elbows on the table and leaned forward.

51

As I was preparing to give my stock description of the lab's clients and testing, a shriek interrupted us. "Adriana, darling! Look Marco, here's Adriana."

A couple descended on our table. The woman, wearing a sleek fur and enveloped in a cloud of perfume, embraced Adriana. The dapper man with her kissed Adriana's cheek and called to the waiter, who brought over two more chairs, menus, and place settings.

As things settled down, Adrianna introduced me to Renata and Marco Gardini. They passed me over as not stylish enough for her and not glamorous enough for him. They didn't appear to notice anything familiar about me, so I assumed they never met Nicole.

"Darling, it's been so long." Renata patted her red flip hairdo. Lowering her voice, she asked, "How is everything going with you?"

"Just fine. I am performing again in April." Adriana smiled brightly.

Marco caused more confusion by recommending what were the best dishes. He took over the ordering, demanding a different wine than what Adriana and I were drinking.

"Trust me, this Barolo wine is much better. We once visited the winery in Italy, the Piedmont region."

Not liking red wine, I didn't bother looking at the label.

Several times Renata tried to continue the conversation in Italian, but Adriana replied in English. I thought it was for my benefit.

"Adriana, we saw Gino this summer. He asked about you. He was so concerned." She winked. "You should call him."

I watched a faint expression of annoyance cross Adriana's face and this time she replied in Italian. I didn't understand. Her answer was abrupt and final. Looking embarrassed Renata brought up a new subject.

"How are Maria and her dear mother? I haven't seen them in ages."

"Maria is fine, and Aunt Sophia is in good health but slowing down. She is eighty-five you know."

Renata dramatically waved her wine glass. "How time flies, it seems like just yesterday we were all in Milan together; you, Maria, Sophia, and your wonderful mother."

The lunch continued with Marco dominating the conversation. During a long, tiresome story of an event that took place during their last trip to Italy, I caught a brief look of boredom and sadness on Adriana's face, and wondered if her thoughts were of the times in the past when she performed and lived with her lover, Nicole.

At last the meal was over. Renata and Marco had a car and insisted on taking Adriana home. Marco called for the check and paid amidst dramatic exchanges with the waiter. Adriana excused herself to walk to the entrance with me.

"I am so sorry we didn't have any time together. Renata and Marco are old family friends. We haven't seen each other for a long time."

"Of course, I understand, they were so happy to see you."

Reflecting my thoughts, she added, "Another time would have been better." Smiling she reached out and fastened the top button of my coat. "It's getting cold out. Does your car have a heater?"

"Not much of one." I didn't want to leave her but reluctantly added. "I should let you get back to them."

"Let's have dinner." She laughed. "We will go where no one knows me. Can I call you?"

"Yes, I would like that." I couldn't wait to see her again and hoped she meant it. I watched Adriana turn and walk back into the dining room. Out on the street, I put my head down and hurried to my car as a strong wind blew in an overcast sky. Driving home, I tried to retain my image of Adriana. I remembered her lovely skin, lustrous hair, dark eyes, charming accent, and her intense expression when she talked. I also recalled her tired and unhappy look.

When I got home, reality set in. Michele would not be happy that our lunch had become a foursome, but maybe Renata and Marco could be a lead, although I doubted it. They certainly didn't fit the White Moon profile.

Chapter Nine

Because of the prospect of our upcoming dinner engagement, Michele forgot her disappointment about the lunch. The agency knew all about Renata and Marco, who had an import business and regularly traveled to Italy. They were what Adriana had said they were—old family friends.

"They are not who we are after. We want to know about any of the women she has contact with. You know what we are looking for." Michele leaned back in her chair, crossing her arms, and giving me a severe look.

Feeling like she just reprimanded me as if I were a naughty schoolchild and to change the subject, I asked, "Who are Maria and Sophia? Some relatives?"

"Sophia is Desi's aunt, her mother's older sister, and Maria is the daughter, her cousin. Maria is ten years older and traveled with Desi until she met Nicole Chapman."

Michele shuffled some papers on her desk and then looked up at me. "What are your plans for Christmas?"

"None right now." Why did she ask?

Michele looked thoughtful while I sat hoping for a reply, but instead she examined her watch. "I have an appointment. Keep me informed about the dinner." She stood and our meeting ended.

Driving uptown, I looked at the Christmas decorations everywhere, and the harried faces of the people crowding the sidewalks. Christmas was almost here, not that it mattered to me. I often wondered if the agency chose me because I had no family. If I disappeared who would care? The tense mood of the upcoming holiday had even infiltrated the agency where, today, Michele had seemed preoccupied and abrupt. I really knew nothing about her personal life and doubted that I ever would. I didn't even know if she was married. She didn't wear any rings on her left hand, but wore a gold band with some engraved design on her right hand. Although our meetings at the agency were always all business and impersonal, I thought she was an attractive woman, and often wondered what she was like away from the agency. Did she even have a life outside the agency?

That night, while lying on the couch reading a book on chess moves, a game I never managed to master, I heard my phone ringing and jumped to answer it.

"Kathryn, this is Adriana. I know this is short notice, could we have dinner together tomorrow night?"

"That would be fine, Adriana." Any night would be fine.

"I just can't believe Christmas is so close. Do you have a place in mind?"

"How about Angelina's in the West Village?" This was the Italian restaurant where Carmen and I had dinner together. I didn't think it was chic enough for Renata and Marco.

"That sounds good. Is seven all right for you?"

"Seven is fine" I answered. "I'll meet you there"

I hung up excited at the thought of Adriana wanting to meet me for dinner. I had been unsure if she would ever call me, but she had.

Before I went back to my book, I decided to call Carmen. I hadn't heard from her as she promised. I paged through my address book until I found her name, and dialed her number. After six unanswered rings, I hung up, intending to try again after Christmas.

†

I arrived at Angelina's first. Warm and dimly lit, with little white lights strung everywhere, candles flickering on the tables, and soft Christmas music playing, it provided just the kind of intimate atmosphere I hoped for.

When Adriana gracefully crossed the room to the table, it struck me again how beautiful she was, and I could picture her on the opera stage in one of her roles. Tonight she wore black slacks and some kind of soft sweater in a shade of plum, and around her neck hung a silver chain with a yellow stone. She draped her coat over the back of her chair, sat across from me, and took my hand in hers.

"Thank you for meeting me on such short notice. I felt badly about my friends interrupting our lunch, and wanted to see you again. Soon."

"I'm so glad you called me," I said, thrilled by her touch and flattered by her words.

She leaned back, smiling as the waiter brought water and the wine list. After looking over the wine list I asked her to select a bottle of wine for us.

"This is nice. I like this place." She looked around her and then turned back in time to catch my eyes lingering on her breasts.

I could feel my face flushing and changed the subject. "Is that necklace amber?"

She looked down at the stone and held it out with her fingers. "Yes, this is Baltic amber, millions of years old I understand. It belonged to my mother."

"It must be amazing to own something that old." Then I remembered I had a piece of a meteorite, which was even older. I thought about mentioning it but didn't, afraid it might sound like bragging.

The wine arrived and the waiter hovered anxiously as Adriana tasted the wine and nodded her approval. He filled our glasses and left. "This is good. I hope you like it, Kathryn." She lifted her glass in a toast and I followed.

"Are you a native New Yorker?" She set her glass down and tilted her head. "You don't sound like one."

I took a deep breath and told her what was true about my life. "I've lived here for three years." She waited for me to continue. "I'm from the Midwest. Wisconsin, but this is my home for now"

"Do you have family back in...Wisconsin?"

"I had an aunt but she died a few years ago." My Aunt Emma died alone in her nursing home while I was overseas. A continuing source of guilt for me.

"So you are alone."

I looked up to see an expression on her face that I could only describe as tender. I swallowed and tried to think of a flippant reply but none came. I simply answered, "Yes."

Our appetizers arrived and, after tasting hers, she gestured toward her plate. "This shrimp is quite good. Would you like to try one?"

"Well, yes please." I waited awkwardly as she placed a shrimp on my plate, and then tipped her head and watched as I ate it.

She smiled. "What do you think? Isn't that good?"

I smiled back. "It's great, a good choice." I would have eaten anything she put on my plate.

We pushed our appetizer plates away as the entrees arrived. Adriana picked up her knife and fork. "This lab where you work, what is it called?"

"Dyna Lab." I grinned. "We call it the dynamite lab."

She put her head back, laughed at my lame joke, and poured more wine into my glass. "Do you like your work?"

"I did in the beginning, but now, unless we acquire a new instrument or set up a new procedure the work is all very routine." This was more of the truth.

She frowned. "They don't make you work on the holiday, do they?"

I shook my head. "No, the lab is closed on Christmas Day."

I decided to turn the conversation away from myself and find out more about her. I pushed my pasta around.

"What do you like to do when you aren't rehearsing or performing?" I laid down my fork, put my hand on my chin, anxious to hear about her personal life.

She ran a hand through her hair and looked across the room, frowning in concentration. "When I have free time, I like to take long walks in Central Park, it's good exercise. When I stay home, I love to read mystery novels." She looked back at me, smiling. "I like to try to figure out who did it."

I wondered if she had enjoyed these simple pleasures with Nicole.

"The detective had this pet cat that helped her solve the crime. Can you imagine that?" She leaned back in her chair laughing. Adriana was telling me the plot of a mystery novel she had recently read and enjoyed. Listening to her gentle voice and looking into her expressive eyes, I knew that the demanding prima donna of my imagination did not exist. Nor was this woman the leader of a terrorist group.

The waiter cleared our table, poured the remainder of the wine into our glasses, and laid down the dessert menu. When he left, Adriana asked, "You said you have no family. Do you have plans for Christmas?"

"Oh, I have friends, we usually do something together." It was not true this year. My friends were couples, and after Kitty left me, I didn't fit in with them.

"Every year on Christmas Day, I have a family open house with Maria and Sophia. Everyone we know is welcome. Could you come? Anytime from two to six. We have excellent food, Maria is a superb cook." She added eagerly, "You could bring your friends."

"That would be wonderful if I weren't intruding." As excited as I was, I knew Michele would be ecstatic about my invitation to Adriana's home on Christmas Day.

She reached over and put her hand over mine. "I want you to come, I will be expecting you. Here, let me give you my address and my phone number." She took a pen from her purse and wrote them on a cocktail napkin.

I took it from her not wanting the evening to end. Perhaps Adriana felt the same because, as we left the restaurant, she paused and looked at me. "Let's come here again, Kathryn. This was a lovely evening for me." I saw her happy, relaxed expression, so unlike the lunchtime at Bella, and hoped I had a part in it.

Adriana left in a taxi, waving goodbye, and I looked forward to spending Christmas Day with her.

Chapter Ten

I tightened the scarf around my neck against the cold as I made my way along the sidewalk, through the crowds and past brightly decorated shops. On the day before Christmas Eve, I was out searching for a Christmas gift to take to Adriana. Not knowing her tastes, I agonized over what to buy. At a wine shop I bought a bottle of good Italian wine. In an import store, I found the present I wanted, a pair of amber earrings with the same antique style silver setting and light yellow hue as her necklace.

I leaned over the showcase and pointed to the earrings. "May I see those? They are for a Christmas gift."

The clerk spread the earrings on a velvet cloth so I could examine them and adjusted her bifocals. "You know amber is of organic, not mineral origin. These are Baltic amber, the fossilized resin from prehistoric evergreens that flourished in large forests, as far back as fifty million years ago." She added, "These are lovely and a good choice as a gift."

I was suitably impressed. "I'll take them." Carrying the wine and my gift-wrapped present I went home. Other than something for my neighbor, Pat, there was no one else to buy presents for this year.

†

Christmas Eve day a party atmosphere prevailed in the lab. Elaborate Christmas cookies and other treats covered the table in the break room, and the aroma of coffee brewing filled the air. My contribution was a ready-made cheese tray. A slow work day encouraged an endless parade back and forth to the break room, and several workers arranged to leave early. I planned to stay all day.

At my workstation, I tried to concentrate on my duties as memories of Adriana Desi's lovely face, her voice, and gestures flooded my thoughts. Reliving the moment when she invited me to her home for the Christmas Day open house, I looked up in time to grab a rack of specimens moving crookedly into the analyzer, narrowly avoiding a jam. I tried not to think of our dinner together as I carefully watched the rack.

"I don't like to interrupt you, but do you think you can see me when you are free?" Startled, I saw Dr. Lan standing next to me. I nervously wondered how long she had stood there. Did she see my inattention when the rack almost jammed?

"Of course." A little behind in my work because of my daydreaming about Adriana Desi, I pointed to the rack of specimens now moving smoothly into the analyzer. "As soon as this batch is finished." Dr Lan nodded and walked away.

This had to be about the lab thefts. Again I wished that I hadn't become involved. Recently, in the break room, Dawn asked me why I was in Dr. Lan's office so much lately. I could see several other co-workers waiting expectantly for my answer, and I didn't want to lie to them, but I really had no choice.

"We're getting ready for a lab inspection this spring. Dr. Lan wants to be sure there are no deficiencies." There would be an inspection, but I had no idea when. Heads nodded, they accepted my answer since no one wanted to fail an inspection.

My work finished, I sat in the office across from Dr. Lan and waited anxiously for her to begin. She picked up a paper clip turning it in her delicate fingers. "I took your suggestion about looking into any recent hires. We do have one, Rob Adams."

I didn't want to tell Dr. Lan as it might sound like gossip, but Rob was a showoff and a pest. The women in the break room were always complaining about him. He was known for trying to get credit for other people's ideas, and on top of that, thought he was irresistible to the women. This was good news. Maybe we could get rid of him. I sat forward eagerly.

"So it was Rob?"

She sighed. "No, unfortunately, the week the columns disappeared he was out sick. I think he had the flu."

What a disappointment. I slumped back in my chair. As Dr. Lan talked, I looked at her trim body and glossy black hair, wondering what she would be like in bed. Would she be as cold and efficient as her lab personality or would she be wildly passionate?

"…don't think there is anyone else," Dr. Lan paused, "Kathryn, are you all right?"

Blinking, I stammered, "Sorry, I was trying to think of some other way to catch this person."

"Yes, well thank you for the suggestion, Kathryn." She managed a slight smile and reached for a logbook.

I nodded. "I'm sorry it didn't work out. I'll watch for anything suspicious." As I left Dr. Lan's office, I felt I let her down and wished there was some way I could help her end this mess.

Back at work, I snapped up my lab coat, determined to concentrate on what I was doing and forget about Adriana Desi and Dr. Lan. At least for now.

In the late afternoon, the paging system announced a call for me. If a client were calling I would be told who it was and what they needed. Suspecting a personal call, I picked up the phone

"Hi Kat. I knew you would be slaving away today."

"Well. We are a little short staffed," I answered coolly. Kitty used to tease me about my industriousness, never calling in sick, always available for weekends.

"So, any plans for dinner tonight?" How did she know I didn't have any? I could easily be with someone new. In the silence that followed, I tried to decide whether or not to make up something.

"The Chinese restaurant is open, I called them. Just the place for Christmas Eve dinner. How late do you work?"

"Until five." Why did I tell her that?

"I'll come to your place about seven. We can walk over."

"I don't think it would be a good idea. There is no reason for us to see each other," I said, thinking this would end it.

Undeterred, Kitty replied. "Oh come on, it's just a meal in a Chinese restaurant."

"I guess you're right."

"Great. I'll pick you up around seven."

I hung up with mixed feelings. It was Christmas Eve and I really didn't want to be alone. But why was Kitty calling me? Where was the doctor?

†

A little after seven, Kitty arrived wearing tan corduroy slacks, black leather boots, and an expensive, lamb's wool sweater. I couldn't see that she had gained any weight. In fact, she looked pretty good as she tossed the bag she was carrying on a chair along with her jacket.

"Here's a bottle of your favorite wine." Kitty thrust a bag at me. "I thought we'd have a glass before we go to the restaurant."

I hadn't planned on entertaining her, and as I grudgingly took the wine to the kitchen I wondered why I didn't just arrange to meet her at the restaurant. I opened the wine and brought the glasses, handing one to Kitty. She raised hers.

"Merry Christmas, Kat."

I briefly toasted her and asked casually, "Where's the doctor?"

Kitty peered into her glass. "Went home to visit her family. Altoona, Pennsylvania. She'll be back tomorrow night."

Evidently Mary Beth's family didn't know about Kitty. Not much of a Christmas for either of them. I might have known there was a reason Kitty called me. What kind of a relationship was that when they couldn't even spend Christmas together?

Looking around my living room with her lively brown eyes, she grinned. "Looks about the same, a little bare though." She pointed at the tree on the table. "Cute little tree makes it look like Christmas."

I owned the few possessions I liked or needed, along with my books. I'd come to a point in my life where I realized that acquiring too much would make it more difficult if I had to move. There was always a chance the agency would reassign me to another city.

Kitty examined my bookcase. "You still have the cat on a pillow. I always liked it." She picked up a small silver sculpture of a cat reclining on a patterned cushion with a tassel at each corner. The shorthaired cat had a smug look and a bell around its neck. It was old and had belonged to my Aunt Emma. Sometime in its life one of the tassels had broken off and been lost. Despite this, I cherished it.

Kitty put the sculpture down, turned away, and picked up the Adriana Desi album. "Are you an opera fan now?" Smiling broadly she added, "Wow, good looking woman."

"Someone recommended the recording," I mumbled, resenting her handling Adriana's recording. Why did I let her come here and roam around the apartment as if she still lived here? It was a mistake and all I wanted was for her to leave.

She continued looking at Adriana's photo and then set it down. "Still play the recorder?"

"Yes, but I think our recorder group is going to break up. Chris doesn't want to continue any longer."

"The little dyke? Can't you find someone to replace her? I know you like playing, that's a shame." In the past Kitty attended several of our concerts. Support for me, not love of early music.

Kitty changed the subject. "How's your novel coming?"

"It's not. I lost interest." To pass the lonely hours in my Thai village, I began writing a mystery novel. After returning to New York, I enrolled in a college writing program. My instructor thought I had talent and that the story was promising. I realized that I had much to learn about the craft of writing, and worked hard on the novel with Kitty's encouragement. Now the manuscript lay in a briefcase in the closet, where I put it after Kitty left me.

"Why don't you work on it?"

"I would need to get a computer. The typewriter is obsolete." I didn't want to discuss the novel. There were too many memories.

"I can help you pick out a computer. Just let me know."

We sat in silence and then Kitty picked up the bag, pulled out a large gift-wrapped box and handed it to me. "For you."

I hadn't thought of exchanging presents and, dismayed by her gesture, I unwrapped the box. Inside I saw a running jacket made of beautiful, lightweight, weather-resistant material, in a lovely shade of blue. Just the kind she knew I would like.

I sat there holding it, not wanting to accept anything from Kitty, but not wanting to appear rude and refuse it.

"Try it on," Kitty urged me.

I put it on. Of course it fit perfectly.

Kitty took a drink of her wine and gave me a seductive look. "You look great."

I took the jacket off and put it back in the box. "Just a minute."

In my bedroom I opened a dresser drawer, took out the small box in its Christmas wrapping. As I stood holding it I couldn't believe I was doing this. How had I let her come into my life again like this? I returned to the living room and handed the box to Kitty. "Here. Merry Christmas."

Kitty looked puzzled as she opened the box. Inside was a gold bracelet she once admired when we were shopping together, still in the wrapping from last Christmas.

She took it out, recognized it, and was quiet for a minute.

"Come over here and put it on for me." She held it out.

I sat down on the couch next to her and fumbled with the clasp, finally hooking it. Kitty leaned over, gently kissed my cheek, and then put her hand behind my head moving her lips to mine. I found myself responding as she held me. It had been so long and yet was still so thrilling. Her fingers found the top button of my shirt. She unbuttoned it and then her hand was in my shirt on my breast. I closed my eyes. Her touch was achingly familiar. I reluctantly pulled away, I couldn't do this.

"Please don't." Whatever her relationship was with the doctor, Kitty was still with her and I had promised the agency I was not involved with anyone.

I turned away, buttoned my shirt, and tried to regain my composure. Kitty leaped from the couch and took the empty glasses to the kitchen as if she were the hostess.

Angry with myself for giving in to her I grabbed my jacket from the closet.

"Let's go." I marched toward the door.

Undaunted, Kitty talked cheerfully of office politics at her job as we walked the few blocks to Yen Chen in the cold evening air, while I tried to forget what had just happened in my apartment.

We were seated, handed the menus, and ordered a glass of wine and our meal. There was no need to open the menus. Long ago we both decided on our favorite dishes and always placed the same order. It was one of the small ways we felt comfortable with one another, knowing what the other liked. I pushed the thought from my mind. Those days were over.

"I started graduate school in the fall." Kitty rearranged the fork and spoon in front of her.

I looked up in surprise. "You did? I didn't know. You didn't tell me when I saw you in the bar."

"Masters in Computer Science. It's a little rough now. I had to cut some of my teaching hours, and with the tuition expenses, I'm looking for a cheaper apartment."

After she left me Kitty moved uptown, to be nearer the doctor. I wondered if the doctor offered her any financial help. It didn't matter because Kitty would never accept it, nor would she ask her rich parents in California for help. She was too independent. I knew one thing. She was not moving in with me.

"I admire you. In the end it will be worth it." I smiled at her. "You won't have any trouble with the courses. You were always pretty smart." Changing the subject, I asked, "What's new with Jan and Linda?" They were the couple we traveled with when returning home from the Peace Corps.

Kitty made a face. "They broke up."

"What?" But then I thought that if this news surprised me, they must have been just as surprised when they heard Kitty and I were no longer together.

"I don't see them anymore. It was awkward because I didn't want to take sides. Anyway, Linda took a job in

Philadelphia, or maybe it was Pittsburgh, and Jan is living in Ohio. I guess she met someone from there." Kitty arranged the napkin under her wine glass. "So, how's your job going?"

"A little stressful right now. Someone has been stealing from the lab and I'm trying to help Dr. Lan find that person."

Kitty laughed. "The exotic Dr. Lan. How does she know someone is stealing?"

My first months at the lab, I talked about Dr. Lan so much that Kitty jokingly accused me of having a crush on her. "She has records of what is missing and when it disappeared." I wanted to defend Dr. Lan.

Kitty frowned. "Sounds serious. I'm not sure I want to see you involved."

"It's too late, I already am. I want to help her." I looked away wanting to stop the talk of Dr. Lan.

Kitty picked up her wine glass and looked at me appraisingly. "Too bad you were always so independent."

Startled, I asked, "Me?" She had it backward. She was the independent one.

"You never really needed anyone, you could live anywhere, do anything. You just adapt and nothing nor anyone affects you." She finished her wine and set the glass aside.

I shook my head. "That's nonsense." The food arrived and we dropped the subject and ate our meal.

Outside the restaurant I turned up my jacket collar and pulled on my gloves. "Goodbye, Kitty. Good luck with your classes and finding an apartment." I meant this as a final goodbye.

Kitty lingered on the sidewalk and then turned away. "Bye, Kat."

As I walked home I thought about her words in the restaurant. Maybe I didn't know myself after all.

Chapter Eleven

The door to Adriana Desi's Upper West Side apartment opened and a small woman with graying dark hair and bright black eyes stood staring at me.

"Hello, I'm Kathryn Austin." I stood there awkwardly, holding my gift-wrapped wine bottle. She recovered gracefully.

"Please come in, let me have your coat. I am Maria, Adriana's cousin." She took my coat as I slipped the small gift box out of the pocket.

We stepped into a spacious, high-ceilinged living room, filled with people standing in groups talking and laughing. I hadn't planned on seeing so many guests for what I thought would be a small family celebration. Across the way, Adriana, looking stylish in an emerald green, silk pantsuit, came toward me. For a wild moment I expected her to embrace me, but she only put her hand on my arm.

Before coming, I had debated at length on what to wear. I decided on nothing too elaborate, but not too casual. Finally I chose black, light wool slacks, and a red cashmere, turtleneck sweater, and I added the antique gold bracelet that had belonged to my aunt.

"Merry Christmas, Kathryn, I'm so glad to see you. What a lovely sweater." She smiled her charming, warm smile, making me feel like I was the only guest in the room.

"What's this, for me?" She laughed and touched the obviously wrapped bottle of wine. "Maria, please take this. How nice of you, Kathryn."

Maria disappeared with the wine and Adriana took my arm as we crossed the room together. "Come see the tree. Not real I'm afraid," she motioned toward the tree, "some fire regulations, I guess."

Great strides had recently been made in the reproduction of Christmas trees, and weighed down by lights, ornaments, garlands, and icicles, it looked warmly realistic.

"This is for you. Merry Christmas." I handed her the small package and waited self-consciously as she unwrapped my gift.

Adriana was silent for a moment and then looked up at me. Was she seeing Nicole? Had she once given her a present like this? Then she smiled warmly and held up the earrings. "To match my amber necklace. How lovely and so thoughtful of you. I'm going to put them under the tree here." She bent down and put the box near the trunk of the tree among some other presents. "Thank you, Kathryn."

Standing, she looked around. "Did you bring your friends?"

In a burst of candor I blurted, "I really had no plans for today."

She looked back at me as I nervously waited for her reply. "Then I'm especially glad you came." She gently took my arm putting me at ease. "Let me introduce you to some of my guests."

Across the room, a handsome dark-haired man waved his wine glass. "Adriana, darling, over here."

I saw a brief look of annoyance as she waved back. "In a moment, Ricardo." She led me over to a tiny old lady seated in a large chair upholstered in heavy dark tapestry. "This is my Aunt Sophia."

Adriana spoke to her in Italian and I recognized my name. I carefully shook her frail hand and wished her a Merry Christmas while she nodded and responded in Italian.

Adriana led me away and we made the rounds of some of her guests. Jack, her manager, a stressed-looking man with a large, dark mustache, wearing a heavy red pullover, stopped talking briefly for the introduction. He shook my hand and then turned back to his captive audience, gesturing nervously as he continued talking. On the other end of the room, I saw Renata and Marco in an animated conversation with another couple. Maria joined us, bringing me a glass of wine, and pointing out the array of food laid out on a long, heavy table in the adjoining dining room.

"Please, go and help yourself." She moved away, and Adriana excused herself to greet a young couple just arriving.

I wandered over to a grand piano holding an assortment of photos. As I examined them, a woman who had earlier been introduced as an Arts Editor for some publication whose name I didn't catch, approached me.

"Have we met before? You look familiar."

She had a pleasant, intelligent face, short wavy blonde hair, and expensive clothes. She must have seen Nicole with Adriana at some time. No one else in this group seemed to find me familiar, so I had an idea that Adriana and Nicole had conducted their relationship discreetly.

"No, I don't think so. I haven't known Adriana very long."

She cocked her head and looked at me. "Are you in the music world?"

"I'm a chemist."

"How interesting." Before she could question me further, someone called to her from a group gathered nearby. "Sorry, maybe we can talk later." She walked away.

"Have you eaten anything?" I turned around to see Maria standing behind me, wearing the same cool look as when I arrived. "I suppose you know you look like Nicole."

"Adriana said I look like someone she knew."

"How did you meet Adriana?" Maria narrowed her dark eyes.

"Outside a bookstore in the rain, she couldn't get a taxi. I gave her a ride."

"What do you do? Adriana said you were a scientist of some kind." Maria had less of an accent than Adriana.

"I work as a chemist in a drug testing lab." Maybe she could tell me something about Nicole.

"Sounds like interesting work."

I shrugged. "Sometimes. May I ask, how did Adriana meet Nicole and who was she?"

Maria tightened her lips and looked across the room. "Adriana always wanted a dog, but with all the travel, and then the last years when her mother wasn't well, it just wasn't possible. Adriana liked to walk in Central Park, and one day she met this woman with a small dog who let Adriana play with it."

Maria took a sip from her glass of red wine and continued. "She went back hoping to see the dog and they met several times after that, but one day the woman didn't have the dog. They went for a drink together and one thing led to another." She added with disgust. "I found out later it wasn't even her dog, but belonged to a friend. I don't think Adriana ever saw the dog again."

"What happened to Nicole?"

"She died in a car accident," Maria said without emotion.

"How tragic."

Maria ignored my comment.

"How old was Nicole?"

"Thirty when she had the accident. They were together less than a year. How old are you?"

"Thirty-two." I waited for Maria to go on with her story.

"Adriana met her at a vulnerable time; her mother had died a year before. Adriana's life was always devoted to her career and her mother. Now she has some time for herself."

I decided to ask a few personal questions. "Have you lived here long?"

"Mother and I came to the states five years before Adriana. I worked as a secretary for an import firm, but when Adriana's career became so successful, I quit so I could travel as her companion."

"Then Nicole went with her instead." I took a chance on this remark.

"Yes, but Adriana always took care of her family. Mother and I have lived here with Adriana since Nicole died."

I understood Maria's initial resentment of me. She thought I was another Nicole poised to take Adriana from her again.

"I appreciate you and Adriana inviting me here today. You've made this a nice Christmas for me," I said sincerely.

"Don't you have any family?"

"No, I don't."

Maria looked at me with less of the coolness she had exhibited earlier. "You may look like Nicole, but you aren't like her. I have to go see about more food. Eat something now." She pointed her wine glass toward the table laden with food and then headed to the kitchen.

Now, as even Maria compared me to Nicole, I knew I could never replace her. More confusing was trying to reconcile the image of a woman who loved dogs, always wanted one, and yet gave the order to abandon the farm, leaving the cats and dogs to starve to death.

The crowd was thinning and I decided it was time for me to leave. I found Maria in the kitchen putting food away in refrigerator containers. "Thank you for having me in your home, Maria."

She wiped her hands on a towel. "Come see us again." She seemed to mean it.

Adriana got my coat and walked me to the door. "I love the earrings. I'll wear them the next time we go to dinner." She reached out and put her hand on my arm. "Kathryn, I hope this has been a good Christmas for you."

As I felt the soft touch of her hand on my arm I could hardly speak, but managed to stammer, "Yes, it has. Thank you so much for inviting me."

On the way home I thought about Maria's attitude toward Nicole. It seemed she didn't like her, but then Nicole had taken her place with Adriana, so of course she resented her. And what did Maria mean when she said I wasn't like Nicole? What was Nicole like? Was she glamorous, flamboyant, and affectionate with Adriana? Was she everything I was not?

That evening back in my apartment I sat down to a task I dreaded doing. I compiled a list for Michele of the names of everyone I knew who had been at the party.

Chapter Twelve

The next afternoon at the agency, Michele put on her glasses, took my list, and examined it.

"Other singers, her manager, writers, family friends." She looked up. "No younger women were there?" I saw the disappointment on her face.

"A few, but they were singers, people she had worked with."

"I guess I didn't really expect she would be seen with any White Moon members in front of her friends and family. When you become closer to her, we expect you can learn more. She may even try to recruit you." She leaned forward. "Has she ever asked you about your political beliefs?"

"No, she never has." Eagerly, I added, "I did find out from Maria how Adriana met Nicole. She was walking in the park. Nicole had a little dog that Adriana liked to play with. She went back there several times to see Nicole and the dog."

Before I could continue Michele interrupted me. "Oh really, Kathryn. Don't you see that's the story she told Maria? Of course she had to cover up how she recruited Nicole." Michele impatiently pushed my list aside.

"In the meantime we have another assignment, short-term, and exactly suited to you."

Michele opened a folder and spread out the papers. "A group of Dutch musicians had a piece of their luggage stolen at Dulles International Airport last week. The case contained a collection of priceless recorders. They turned up yesterday at a music store in Washington, D.C., where two men tried to sell them, but were instead persuaded to leave them on consignment."

She handed me a list of the recorders and I looked it over. It included a handmade Renaissance consort and double bass in baroque tuning, expensive and rare instruments.

Michele continued. "The Royal Netherlands Embassy contacted us and we are working with them to recover these items. We want you to fly to Washington the day after tomorrow, and pose as a shop assistant. When the thieves turn up for their money, you will call our agents and have them arrested. We have arranged everything with the music store owner, who is expecting you. At work tomorrow, ask for time off. Say your aunt is in town unexpectedly and you want to spend time with her and show her around."

Michele handed me a thick envelope. "Your plane ticket, hotel reservation, and instructions." After a pause she added, "Good luck on your assignment, Kathryn."

✝

Two mornings later at the airport, I approached the security gate and showed my identification. The Security Screener at the gate called the Checkpoint Security Supervisor who came over and led me around the gate. My weapon would set off the metal detector so I wasn't subjected to a hand wanding.

I arrived in Washington, checked into my hotel, unpacked my few things, and then took a taxi to the Melville Music Store.

Overwhelmed, I looked around me at a huge display of drums, a selection of electric guitars, amplifiers of all sizes, pianos, and keyboards. Trumpets, trombones, French horns, and saxophones were displayed on the walls, while cases held flutes, clarinets, and their accessories. A separate humidified room contained violins, other string instruments, and acoustic guitars. Rows of bins and shelves along one wall held music and instruction books.

The owner, John Melville, a large man with a reddish beard and pink face, came out of his office to shake my hand and greet me. It was early afternoon with only a few customers in the store.

We sat in his office and he leaned back in his chair as it creaked dangerously. "These two guys came in here and asked Tyler if this was a music store. Can you believe that?" He gestured around him at the store crowded with instruments, and added proudly, "This is the only full-service music store in Washington, D.C. Besides the instruments, we offer rentals, lessons, and repairs."

I waited for him to go on.

"Tyler Nordstrom is my manager. They asked him to come out to their car to see these recorders in the trunk. They wanted a thousand dollars for the recorders, but Tyler told them he would have to find a buyer, and convinced them to leave the recorders with our store. I only carry a few student models so I called a well-known area player and asked him to come have a look. He knew about the theft and recognized the instruments." His chair tipped forward and landed with a thud. "We called the Netherlands Embassy and here you are."

Next I met Tyler, a tall, intense, blond young man in tan slacks and a blue, oxford cloth shirt. He shook my hand and looked around the store.

"Kathryn, we'll have you doing a few tasks like stocking and arranging things, or if you prefer, you can just hang out in John's office. I told the men I would need a few days to find anyone interested in buying the recorders, so I expect them to come back anytime now."

Early that evening I sat eating alone in the hotel restaurant. Looking around, I saw another woman and two men also eating alone, while bland arrangements of old Broadway hits played in the background, accompanied by the muted clatter of dishes and silverware. Lonely and self-conscious, I hurried through my meal and escaped to my room.

That night I lay on the bed and wondered what I was doing here in a strange city, waiting for two thieves to show up—who knew when? I thought about Kitty's arms around me, her lips on mine, and what might have happened if I hadn't stopped her. Nothing would have changed, I would still be here. She was not going to leave the doctor. And what about Adriana? I suspected that she still saw Nicole when she looked at me. I couldn't replace her and that made me feel depressed and helpless.

The next day was uneventful. I had always found musical instruments of all kinds fascinating and it was enjoyable to be around so many different types, listening to them and handling them. I spent most of my time unpacking and arranging displays. Tyler and the other employees were pleasant to work with, and the store was busy with customers making after-holiday purchases. I spent another lonely night eating in the hotel restaurant, and then returned to my room and lay on my bed, trying to find something of interest on the television.

My third day at the store, as I unpacked and arranged some jazz tune collections for saxophone, I became aware of someone standing next to me.

"Hello, are you new here?"

I looked up to see a tall woman with medium length, dark-red hair and light brown eyes, carrying a brief case, and what looked like a flute case.

"I'm just helping out temporarily. One of John's clerks is on vacation. You know, the holidays."

"I see." She held out her hand for a firm handshake and smiled warmly. "Valerie Patterson. I teach flute here."

"Kathryn Austin." I smiled back as I took her hand.

We both stood there awkwardly and then she looked at her watch. "I have my first lesson now. I'll be here giving lessons for at least another three hours. Will you still be here?"

"Yes, I will"

"Talk to you later."

I watched with interest as she disappeared into the back where the lesson studios were located.

A little over three hours later I saw Valerie Patterson leaving John's office. She turned back to wave to him and then came over to me.

"How's it going? John said you don't live here, just came to help out for a short time over the holiday season."

"Yes, this is my third day. I'm enjoying it."

She looked thoughtful. "I don't know if you have any plans for this evening, but if not, would you like to go for dinner?"

"I would." The thought of another lonely meal in the hotel dining room was depressing.

"Where are you staying?"

"At The Diplomat."

"I know it, nice, and it has a good restaurant, but it's kind of dull. There is a place a few blocks away called Egan's that you might like. Should I meet you about seven in the lobby and we can walk over?"

"Great, I'll look forward to it." I was definitely interested in seeing more of her.

There was another awkward moment and then she adjusted her briefcase strap over her shoulder. "Seven then." She turned and left.

An hour later, before I left the store, John and I sat in his office discussing when the thieves might return.

"Tyler told them he needed a few days to find a buyer so I expected them sooner, especially since New Years is two days away." He swept aside a pile of papers on his desk. "I saw you met Valerie."

"She invited me to dinner tonight. I wasn't sure what to say about my being here. I told her that I was helping out while someone was on vacation."

John thought for a moment. "What you told her is fine." He shifted in his chair. "Valerie has taught here for a long time and is well known and respected in the music community. I think you'll enjoy her company tonight."

Valerie seemed like a nice person, and my job at the agency was already associated with too much deceit, but it was my assignment and she was a stranger.

†

That evening I sat next to Valerie Patterson in the bar of Egan's. Decorated in warm, dark wood and shiny brass, the room had shelf upon shelf of sparkling liquor bottles facing us, while show tunes played softly in the background. Valerie looked attractive, her hair pulled back with a barrette, wearing dark gray slacks and a black sweater, the low neckline showing a little cleavage. A tiny gold cross dangled on a chain around her neck. I wore my black slacks with a gray cashmere turtleneck sweater.

Valerie picked up her martini. "John was lucky to find you to help him. Did you know him before coming here?"

Valerie wasn't what is considered conventionally pretty, but rather handsome with her tall slim body, thick red hair, large brown eyes, and pleasant smile. I had a commitment to the agency and it included secrecy about my assignment. "No, someone who knows him told me he could use some help over the holidays. I can only stay a few more days."

"That's very good of you."

We picked up our drinks, mine a glass of white wine, and drank in silence. Feeling uneasy about deceiving her, I hoped she would change the subject.

Valerie turned toward me.

"Are you married, Kathryn?"

"No, I'm not." I decided to tell her more, an abridged version. "I had a partner, but she left me a year ago, just before Christmas."

Valerie set her glass down abruptly almost spilling her drink. "What a shame and how familiar. I had what I thought was a wonderful relationship for seven years. Ten

86

months ago, I came home from a tour with my chamber group and Alicia announced she was leaving me. I couldn't understand what had happened. I often traveled for master classes, recitals, and performances." She frowned into her martini glass. "I don't know, maybe I was gone too much. Anyway, she met someone and they have since moved to Florida. At least we don't have to run into each other."

Unhappy for her, I murmured, "I'm sorry to hear that."

Valerie signaled for another drink. "It took a while, but I'm over it. I don't want another relationship. I can't go through that again." She looked at me. "And you?"

"I'm too busy with my work now." As good an excuse as any, I thought.

So here we were, two women who didn't want to become involved with anyone.

"Should we get a table?" Valerie picked up her drink.

Seated in the dining room, Valerie looked at me over her menu. "I'm looking forward to this next year. I've made the decision to apply for a college position teaching flute. I'm tired of traveling and freelancing. I've come to realize that what I love best is teaching, and there are several positions available right now. I'll have to relocate, but that's fine with me. I want to be part of a community." Smiling shyly she added, "Maybe I could even buy a little house."

"Good for you. Sounds like a wonderful decision." I thought how, unlike me, at least she had a plan for her future.

Valerie closed her menu with a snap. "Enough of this talk about me. Let's see, have you seen any good movies lately?"

We laughed together as the waiter approached our table.

After the meal, while we were lingering over coffee, Valerie picked up her cup. "I'm not teaching at the store until after New Year's. It looks as if you might be here on New Year's Eve."

"I'm not sure. John may not need me after New Year's." I hoped the thieves returned before then.

"You don't want to be alone. Some of us are getting together and having our own party. We didn't want to go to a bar. Anyway, you're invited." She rummaged in her purse and pulled out a business card and a pen.

"My phone number is on this, and I'll also write my address." She turned the card over and began writing.

"Are you sure your friends won't mind?" I had already envisioned a New Year's Eve alone, sitting over a drink in the hotel bar.

"You will be welcomed. I have an answering machine, just leave a message and I can come pick you up."

"I could take a taxi."

"No, it's all right, not a problem." She handed me the card.

As we walked back to the hotel in the cold darkness, Valerie hummed a tune, which I recognized from one of the Mozart flute concertos, while I struggled with a decision. Should I invite her up to my room? If so, it would only be for one purpose. Did I want to? Did she want to?

In a mellow mood after numerous drinks and tasty food, I wasn't sure if my feelings for Valerie were ones of affection or desire.

When we reached the entrance of the hotel, I asked, "Would you like to come up for a glass of wine? I saw some in my room's refrigerator bar." I laughed nervously. "I'm afraid no martinis though."

Valerie hesitated and I saw a fleeting expression of indecision on her face. "Well, yes. Thank you."

In my room she excused herself to use the bathroom. I opened the small refrigerator and took out two miniature bottles of white wine. I set them on the table near the window, and as I unwrapped two plastic glasses, Valerie came up behind me and put her hands on my shoulders. She moved my hair aside and kissed the back of my neck. I felt her warm breath and soft lips. I turned around and pulled her to me, our bodies pressed together, our breasts touching. Our lips met in a tender, tentative kiss.

Valerie drew back slightly. "Kathryn, you are so attractive, but I don't think I..." She faltered and looked as if she would cry.

"It's all right, I understand." Two strands of her hair had escaped the barrette, and I gently pushed them back, and then touched her cheek with my fingers. I stepped back. "How about some of this rare vintage?"

Valerie nodded and attempted a smile. We sat down together at the small round table, and I twisted the caps off and poured our wine. We silently raised our glasses in a toast.

As we drank our wine Valerie relaxed, put her feet up on a stool, and related an anecdote of her travels with her chamber group, while I leaned back, lounging in my chair, enjoying listening to her.

"So here we were, performing in this Civic Auditorium somewhere in Kansas, when they interrupted to announce a tornado warning. Then the lights went out and I thought, 'Oh no, I'm going to be blown away along with my expensive flute.'"

When our glasses were empty Valerie looked at her watch. "I guess I better get going."

"I'll go down with you." In the elevator together we smiled at one another and Valerie reached out and squeezed my hand. "Thank you for the lovely evening."

Outside the entrance to the hotel she took my arm. "Now Kathryn, don't forget about New Year's Eve." She added warmly. "You know you're welcome to join us."

I waited and watched as she walked to the parking lot and got in her car. We waved to each other and I went up to my room.

As I undressed I looked over at the empty bed and thought about the evening. Being with Valerie had been enjoyable and comfortable, but it was best that it ended as it had. A one-night affair would not have been right. She had already been hurt. So had I.

When I fell asleep my dreams were of Adriana Desi.

†

On the morning of the fourth day, the day of New Year's Eve, as I unpacked a shipment of guitar gig bags, two men entered the store. From their awkward behavior and their appearance, I immediately suspected these were the thieves. The taller one wore a scuffed, quarter-length, brown leather jacket, open to show his partially unbuttoned shirt with a heavy gold chain around his neck. His bearded partner wore a grimy team jacket and a Yankees baseball cap. Both men had on sunglasses, although the day was dark and overcast.

I busied myself with a music stand display, letting them wait for Tyler as he rang up a sale of saxophone reeds. When he finished, Tyler approached them. I listened from behind my display.

"You know those recorders you left here? I have good news for you; someone is interested in buying them. Let's go in the office."

They followed him into John's office, and I went to the phone behind the counter to dial the pre-arranged number.

"Hello, the music you ordered has arrived and is ready for pickup." This was the signal for the agency to send a team out to the store.

After I hung up, I went to the office door. "Please excuse me Tyler, but I have a call about the King Single F horn. Is this our final price or can we reduce it?"

"Which one is it? I better take a quick look." He turned to the two men. "Sorry, just a minute, I'll be right back."

"The one on the wall there." I pointed across the room and followed him over to the horn. He examined the price tag.

"The music will be picked up shortly," I whispered.

"Good, take fifty off this price," he announced loudly and then returned to the office. Not sure how promptly the agency's team would arrive, I figured a little delay wouldn't hurt.

About fifteen minutes later the two men came out of the office, followed by Tyler thanking them for their business. They opened the front door and then abruptly slammed it shut. The taller man grabbed the terrified Tyler by the shoulder and spun him around.

"Show us your back door. Get going," he growled, as he pushed Tyler ahead of him.

I expected an easy arrest after my phone call. None of my previous assignments ever involved any real physical risk, but now I had a decision to make as Tyler, stumbling ahead of the men, headed to the back door. What if they got away and took him hostage? My heart was racing as I took several deep breaths to calm myself.

I drew my gun just as they pulled the door open, only to be confronted by more agency police waiting for them. Retreating back into the store, they turned around to find me holding my gun on them. Through the front door came more agency police who promptly handcuffed them and led them away.

After they had left, Tyler sank into the nearest chair. "Geez, Kathryn, thanks. You scared me as much as they did." The color had drained from his face, and beads of perspiration dotted his forehead. I didn't feel much better.

I had already put my gun away and, not having any liquor at hand for either one of us, the best I could do was bring Tyler a glass of water, which he quickly drained.

A half hour later, John, who had been called from his home, sat in the office listening to Tyler's dramatic description of the encounter, as we drank coffee and ate a chocolate cheesecake John brought for us. Tyler had recovered, and happily shoveled a large piece into his mouth.

"I took my time, explaining to them that the instruments were not what most people would want to buy, but luckily I had remembered someone who was always looking for these older ones. I told them it had taken a few days to get in touch with him, and at first he didn't want to pay their price. He relented when I explained I only had them on consignment for a short time."

Tyler picked up another piece of cheesecake and continued the story. "Then I took a long time getting the money and making out a receipt for them to sign. Kathryn helped stall them with an interruption about a horn price inquiry."

As interesting as working in the store had been, with the assignment over I was anxious to go home. Luckily I got a seat on a late afternoon flight. With thanks and goodbyes from John and Tyler, I departed with a gift of some new recorder music.

Before I checked out of the hotel, I left a carefully rehearsed message for Valerie. "Hi, it's Kathryn. I want to thank you for our evening together, I really enjoyed it. I won't be able to come to the party tonight. John encouraged me to go home for New Year's since he won't need me any longer. Anyway, I have an afternoon flight home. Thanks again and Happy New Year, Valerie."

The plane landed that evening in a heavy snowstorm with everything already wearing a blanket of snow. The local weather forecast called for continuing snowfall throughout the night and into the next day.

Around ten that night I arrived at my apartment, unlocked the door, and stomped the snow from my shoes. I entered to the phone ringing, but it stopped before I could reach it. Could it be that the doctor was out of town again and Kitty was calling? Most likely it was someone with too much to drink calling a wrong number.

I wondered about Valerie's New Year's Eve party. Were they all having a good time? Although it had been kind of her to invite me, I just didn't feel like staying in Washington to spend the night with a group of women I didn't know, as nice as they probably were.

I hung up my coat, dragged my suitcase into the bedroom, and took out only what I needed. After I read over my mail, which consisted mostly of bills, I poured a glass of wine and put on the Desi recording. Stretched out on my couch, I managed to stay awake until midnight and then went to bed ready to awaken to a new year, whatever it might hold for me.

Chapter Thirteen

Snow fell all of New Year's Day. In the afternoon, instead of running I put on my hiking boots, ski jacket, knit cap, heavy gloves, and took a long walk in a nearby park. I found the gently falling snow to be light and fluffy— beautiful because I didn't have to be anywhere or shovel it. The few hardy walkers in the park waved to one another and exchanged New Year's greetings. As the light snow fell around me, I wondered if Chris and her friends were planning their ski trip. I really hadn't expected Chris to invite me since it had been an idea of the moment. She had a partner, and her friends didn't know me.

I stopped at Yen Chen on my way home to get a take-out order. It was early in the evening and not too crowded, so I decided to stay and eat there just to be among other people. Once I looked up from my table and panicked when I thought I saw Kitty entering the restaurant, but when the woman turned her head to talk to her companion, I saw that it was someone else. I should have known that even though they were probably together again, the doctor wouldn't come here to eat. Not classy enough.

I wondered about Adriana. Maybe she had been at the Met's New Year's Eve performance and gone out with friends afterwards. Today she would be with her family. When I finished my meal and broke open my fortune cookie, the small piece of paper read: "Travel and romance await you." I set it aside thinking, *how ridiculous*.

At home I set up my chessboard trying to recreate a game from one of my books. A half hour later I lost interest and put on the Desi recording. As I listened to her beautiful voice, I wondered when I would see Adriana again. What would happen when she returned to the opera world? Would she have any time for me? Maybe I would have to think up a reason and this time call her. It was no longer just an assignment. I wanted to be with her.

†

Predicted to end around noon, the snow continued to fall the next morning. Although things were slow at the lab since it was closed New Year's Day, several employees were delayed getting to work, leaving us short staffed so the morning passed by quickly.

While walking in the park the day before, I had come up with another idea which might help Dr. Lan solve her lab theft problem. After lunch I stopped in front of her office. The door was open, and as I peered in she looked up.

"Come in, Kathryn, and take a seat." After I sat down she added, "I hope you had a good holiday season."

"Yes, thank you. I hope you did too." I blushed at the thought of my earlier fantasy of Dr. Lan in bed. I knew she didn't want to hear what I had done over the holidays. It was just polite small talk, and when she didn't mention my absence while I was in Washington, supposedly entertaining my aunt, I again wondered if there was some arrangement with the agency. If so, I was sure I would never know.

"I have thought of something else regarding the thefts."

"Go on."

"Do you keep the work schedules?" These were the weekly work assignments, printed and posted every Monday morning, assigning each worker to a station for a week.

"Yes, I keep them for several months so I can be sure everyone gets to rotate through all the analyzers and other duties on a regular basis." Dr. Lan appeared puzzled at my question.

I eagerly continued. "I was thinking that perhaps you could correlate who was working at that station at the time an item disappeared."

Dr. Lan smiled. It was a rare occurrence. "That is ingenious. I have a log of what was missing and when, and I have the work area assignments."

With nothing more to say I stood preparing to leave. I was pleased with myself because Dr. Lan appeared to like my suggestion.

"Thank you, Kathryn. I will let you know what I find."

As I left her office I thought that it was another stilted conversation between us. One more emotionless exchange, except this time she did smile.

About two in the afternoon the overhead page announced my name for what I knew would be a personal phone call. It had to be Kitty. I picked up the phone and assumed my frostiest tone. "Yes, this is Kathryn Austin."

"Oh, Kathryn, I apologize for interrupting you at work. It is just that I have been trying to call you at home for days."

"I've been...out of town." I was taken by surprise. I couldn't believe Adriana was calling me at work.

"Oh, I didn't know." She paused. "Something has come up and I wonder if we could meet somewhere, perhaps later today."

I sensed the anxiety in her voice. I had completed my specimen workload for the day. Perhaps the fictitious visiting aunt would be useful. "I could arrange to leave work early."

"I just finished a meeting in my manager's office. Could we meet at Bella?"

"I can be there in an hour. Would that be all right?"

"Wonderful. See you there."

I left my work area, approached Dr. Lan's office, and looked in. "I'm sorry to interrupt you but I wonder if I can leave early. This is my aunt's last day in town and I want to take her to an early dinner."

Dr. Lan barely looked up from the papers on her desk. "Yes, Kathryn, you may go."

Sometime in the afternoon the snow had stopped, and now the temperature had dropped. I fastened the top button on my duffle coat, and pulled my knit hat down as I made my way to Bella.

I arrived at Bella first and chose a small table where I could watch for Adriana. When she came in the entrance, wearing a long, expensive-looking fur coat, fur hat, and leather boots, she looked every inch the diva. This was the woman in the glamorous photos.

Approaching the table, she removed her leather gloves and shrugged off her coat. "I am so glad I finally was able to reach you, Kathryn." She sat opposite me twisting her gloves in her hands. The waiter approached our table and she turned to me. "Would you like a glass of wine?"

I nodded. Full of apprehension, I wondered what could be wrong.

The waiter quickly returned with our glasses and Adriana waited for him to move away. "I'm leaving for Paris next week. The Paris Opera has asked me to step in for their performance of *Don Carlo*. The soprano quit. I suspect that, most likely, she was dismissed after she had an argument with the director and quarreled with the conductor."

Shocked, I asked in what I hoped was in a casual voice, "How long will you be gone?"

"At least six weeks."

Six weeks. That was an eternity. I couldn't believe this news.

"Maria was planning to go with me, but Sophia fell and broke her hip."

I frowned at this. "Is she all right?" I knew Adriana must be anxious about leaving her aunt at this time.

"The surgery was three days ago, and we are pleased that she is doing so well. Of course Maria cannot go with me now, and I was wondering if …" She stopped and bit her lip.

I sat anxiously waiting.

"I do not know about your vacation time, or if you are even interested, but I thought maybe you would consider going with me." She sat silently, awaiting my reply.

I couldn't believe it. A chance to go to Paris with Adriana Desi. My next thought was about the agency. Since I was not approved for overseas assignments, I knew they would not allow it. I could ask, plead my case, but the answer would be "no."

When I didn't respond, she added, "I am sure it might be a problem about your job, but perhaps you could think about it and then let me know. I don't want there to be trouble about your work." Adriana picked up her glass of wine, and then set it down without drinking.

I thought, forget the agency, forget the job, this was my life. "I do want to go. Yes, I will go. Never mind the job." I waved my hand in a gesture of dismissal. "I have plenty of vacation time."

She looked surprised, relieved, happy—a mixture of all three. "Are you sure? Do you have a passport? We leave on Tuesday."

"Yes, my passport is up-to-date. I'll arrange something with my job."

"Can you come to dinner at my apartment tomorrow night? Maria will be there and we can talk about the trip."

"I'll be there." Nothing would stop me.

Now she was smiling as we toasted each other. "To our trip. It is so good you can go." She paused. "So good."

After I left her I came back to reality and thought about having to face Michele.

†

As I feared, they rejected my request. Maybe this was an understatement.

"It is absolutely out of the question. You know very well your classification is for limited assignments, which means nothing outside the country." Michele removed her glasses and glared at me. "I certainly hope you didn't make any kind of commitment for this trip."

For the first time since I'd worked for them, I spoke up to her. "Michele, I have a feeling the White Moon members are operating overseas now, probably in Paris. This is a perfect opportunity for us. No one you have over there will be able to get as close to her as I can." I tried to appear objective and detached, appealing to her sense of what was best for the agency

Michele rose and moved to the door trying to regain her usual cool composure. She turned back to me and ordered, "Stay here."

Alone in the windowless room, I stared at an empty desk for what seemed forever.

Twenty minutes later Michele returned carrying some papers and sat down looking slightly subdued. She picked up a pen and tapped it on the desk. I waited.

"It seems that yesterday we received a communication from our agency in Paris, alerting us that they had intercepted a message from the White Moon, announcing their leader here in the states would be arriving in Paris to head an important mission." She tossed the pen aside. "Of course, that has to be Desi."

I sat listening to Michele, unable to believe it was Adriana she was referring to. She was going to Paris for only one reason. To sing in an opera. It seemed to me that the agency had become so obsessed with uncovering the White Moon that they were focusing on an innocent person.

"We took into account your unique position of closeness to Desi. This may present us with the opportunity to expose her, and uncover the other White Moon members that may be operating in Paris, before they do any terrible damage."

She sat back in her chair and crossed her legs. "You are to be constantly in contact with our agents and no freelancing. Is that understood?" She directed a severe look at me.

"Yes, Michele." I was the submissive agent once again.

Appearing satisfied, she added, "We'll go over your instructions in a few days."

I wondered if it was Dr. Caldwell, the Chief of Operations, behind the decision to allow me to go to Paris.

Michele's tone lightened. "By the way, Kathryn, we were pleased with your performance in Washington. You may be interested in knowing that a house call to the gang leader's location turned up another forty suitcases stolen from the airport."

"That's good to hear." They approved of something I had done. A rare occurrence, one not likely to happen again.

Michele was silent as she turned over some papers and then looked at me, frowning. "You haven't been signed into the gym lately."

After Kitty left me, I dropped my membership in the club where we worked out together. Instead, I went to the agency gym, a cheerless place where there were no coffee or juice bars, no casual conversations, and no pickup attempts. I went there, changed, worked out, showered, changed again, and left. Since few women worked out there, I spent a lot of my time readjusting the settings on the circuit training machines. My attendance had been sporadic the past few weeks.

"I guess with the holidays and this assignment, I've been busy." I shifted uneasily in my chair.

Michele appeared to ignore my excuse. "When were you last at the firing range?"

I thought back. "In November, the week of Thanksgiving."

"You know we want a monthly visit. Arrange to go before you leave." Michele sat there looking tired and unhappy, and I wondered how she spent her Christmas, and what she did for New Years. I could speculate forever, I would never know.

✝

The agency's firing range was in another part of the warehouse, and despite the dreary exterior, inside it was quite up to date, with carefully controlled ventilation to pull smoke and lead particles away from the shooting line, and exhaust them from the building. No danger here of lead poisoning as in the old indoor ranges of the past.

I signed in, picked up eye and ear protection, and selected a 9mm Beretta. After settling in, I did pretty well, especially when I envisioned Dr. Mary Beth Neuhausen in the target. Not that I personally disliked her, she didn't even know who I was, but it added a little extra motivation, and when a shot hit the target in the heart I thought, *how appropriate*.

As I left the range and walked to my car in the growing darkness of the late afternoon, I realized the agency only cared that I not do anything clumsy that would expose their search for the White Moon members. With many other agents available to them, they considered me expendable.

Chapter Fourteen

"So then Adriana reached for the knife to stab Scarpia and it wasn't on the table. The most important prop in *Tosca* and they forgot it! She had to pretend she had a knife. Luckily it was the dress rehearsal."

Adriana and I laughed as Maria told this story and others about past trips they had taken together. She also regaled us about some of the more colorful personalities they had met and worked with in former opera performances. Maria was open and friendly with me, and Adriana looked relaxed and casual in jeans and a black turtleneck jersey which emphasized her breasts. I tried not to stare.

Maria had prepared us a good meal of pasta and some kind of eggplant dish that was more than I was accustomed to eating. I noticed Adriana only ate small portions of everything. Later we sat around the table finishing our wine.

"Kathryn, I'm glad we could get together this evening. I have been so busy spending all my time relearning my role in *Don Carlo*."

Maria waved her hand. "Adriana is a quick study and besides she sang the role a few years ago. With great success I might add."

Adriana put down her fork and pushed her plate away. "Elisabetta is a role I truly enjoy singing." She looked happier than I had ever seen her since we met.

"We went on a shopping expedition today." Maria looked over at Adriana. "She needed some new outfits for the trip."

Adriana smiled and swirled the wine in her glass. "Yes, I got some new undergarments."

Maria looked embarrassed. "Well, that too." She got up, taking a stack of plates to the kitchen. "Stay there, I have some special dessert."

While she was gone, Adriana anxiously asked me, "Was there any trouble at your laboratory about you taking the time off?"

"No, I've accumulated a lot of vacation time, and things are slow right now." Why did I have to lie to her? Right now I resented the agency and chastised myself for my deceit.

Adriana looked me over. "Kathryn, do you work out?"

"Yes, I run and go to a gym."

"I thought so. I have a personal trainer. I quit when I wasn't singing last year, but now for the last three months, we have been working together again."

"No wonder you look so good." As soon as the words were out I regretted them. It sounded like a pickup line in a bar.

Adriana did not appear to be offended. "Thank you. In certain opera roles we have to be able to move gracefully, as we fall down and then get up quickly at times." She made a face. "And navigate staircases while singing. I find the trainer very helpful."

We listened to dishes clattering in the kitchen and then Adriana put her elbows on the table and leaned forward. "Maria is so disappointed she can't go to Paris, but she is also pleased you are going with me."

I guessed that getting Maria's approval was an accomplishment. "I understand she has always traveled with you."

"Yes, although last year my friend Nicole went to Paris and London with me. Maria wanted to join us later in London. But she didn't." She paused, glancing in the direction of the kitchen as she added, "I know she wants to be there, but there is very little chance she can come to Paris. You see, Sophia will need to go to a kind of rehabilitation home after she leaves the hospital."

I thought that if she did come it would make Adriana happy. She seemed quite dependent on Maria. I wasn't sure how I felt about this, but I wanted the best for Adriana.

Our dinner together was a success, and I was pleased that Maria appeared to accept me as Adriana's friend. As I left, I looked forward to our trip to Paris together.

†

The next morning I tried calling my agent friend, Carmen. The response was a recorded message informing me that the number was no longer in service. Thinking I might have dialed the wrong number, I tried again and got the same impersonal message. Getting out my address book, I copied her address on a piece of scrap paper and set out to find her.

†

In the East Village, not far from the Italian restaurant, I found Carmen's apartment building, an old, grimy, brick structure sandwiched between a shoe repair shop and a small delicatessen. I entered the cramped lobby and searched the directory for Carmen's name. The nameplate for apartment number 204 was empty.

As I looked at the piece of paper in my hand, a woman entered the lobby. Probably in her forties, she wore a long, bedraggled, fake-fur coat, and a striped, knit, stocking cap with a matching scarf. A loaf of French bread stuck out the top of the grocery bag she carried.

"Excuse me. I'm looking for Carmen Manzano." I waved my piece of paper.

She narrowed her eyes and stared at me. "Are you a friend of hers? If you are, you would know that she doesn't live here anymore."

"I haven't been in touch with her lately. I've been out of town for several weeks."

She jammed her key in the door and said grudgingly. "She's been gone about two weeks. Last week two men came and cleaned out her apartment."

I watched as she entered and slammed the door shut. "Thanks a lot," I murmured.

Out on the sidewalk I looked at the shoe repair shop. Chances were Carmen didn't frequent it, but looking at the deli I thought she must have gone there often.

†

This time of the day was the lull between breakfast and lunch, and the place was empty although the pleasing aroma of fresh coffee and bakery goods filled the air. I approached the counter. A man in his fifties with a bandana on his head, and a short graying beard, looked over my head and asked in a bored voice. "What can I get you?"

"A small coffee and a plain bagel to go." When he dropped the bag on the counter I handed over my money and asked, "Do you know Carmen who lives next door?"

He frowned. "Carmen?" He looked perplexed. "Oh, the dark-haired good-looking gal." He handed me my change. "Haven't seen her lately, probably at least a week. Maybe two."

I persisted. "You didn't hear if she moved away?"

"Hey, in this neighborhood they come and go. Next!" He looked beyond me where a line of two people had formed. I picked up my bag and turned away as the elderly woman behind me glared at me for holding her up.

Back in my car I put the unwanted coffee and bagel on the floor. What had happened to Carmen? Maybe the agency had assigned her to a location out of state and she had given up her apartment. I hoped this was the case. I had a bad feeling about her disappearance.

†

Now that the agency had approved my trip to Paris, Michele moved swiftly ahead with the plans. At our final meeting she handed me a piece of paper printed with a French recipe for cassoulet and pointed, with a well-manicured finger, to the extensive list of ingredients.

I kept my hands in my lap. My nails were clean and trimmed, but my cuticles needed some attention. I mentally put it on my list of things to do before I left for Paris.

"These numbers comprise the telephone number of the agency in Paris." She indicated the number for the amount of each ingredient. "Call as soon as you arrive and they will give you directions." She pointed further down the recipe. "It's a travel agency and this line is the response they will expect from you for further identification."

I imagined the travel agency to be a front similar to the employment agency here. After all the directives regarding my trip were covered, I had a request of my own. "I would like secure indoor storage for my car while I'm gone."

Michele looked surprised and somewhat annoyed that I would ask for anything personal. She quickly jotted something on a legal pad in front of her.

"All right, we can arrange it. I'll have someone come by for it." She rolled the pen in her fingers. "What is your relationship with your co-workers? Are you close enough to anyone that they know anything about your family?"

"No, no one." Why did she ask this?

"Good. Then the explanation for your absence from the lab will be that your mother, back in Wisconsin, is scheduled for hip replacement surgery. You are going to take a leave to go back there and care for her."

I nodded. "All right." More deception. I changed the subject. "By the way, Adriana said there is a slight possibility Maria may join us later in Paris. Her mother is going to a nursing home after the hospital, so I don't think it will happen."

Michele looked thoughtful. "I wouldn't think Desi would want her there, making it difficult to meet with White

Moon members. But, I suppose she is used to working behind her back. We'll see what happens."

Michele took off her glasses and looked directly at me. I noticed for the first time that she had lovely green eyes. "Kathryn, I was against you going to Paris. I think it will be too dangerous for you." There was an awkward silence and then she put her glasses back on.

I remembered Carmen's concern about her assignment. "Michele, do you know where Carmen Manzano is? She was going to call me before Christmas and I haven't heard from her. Her phone has been disconnected and her apartment is empty." I sat holding the recipe waiting for her answer.

"You know we don't give out information about other agents." Michele briskly picked up the pile of papers on her desk.

"But, how can I find out?"

"I told you …" Michele dropped the papers and looked down at them. She lowered her voice. "Something went wrong with her assignment. Carmen is dead. I'm sorry, Kathryn."

I sat in stunned silence as Michele rose and extended her hand. I stumbled to my feet.

"I wish you luck in Paris," she added softly. "Please be careful."

I left her office overwhelmed by the news of Carmen's death. Like me, Carmen had no family and I wondered if the agency chose her for that reason.

Chapter Fifteen

The next morning in the lab, I checked the schedule to see that my assignment for the day had become a project. This could be anything from reviewing a procedure to researching a technical subject. I reported to Dr. Lan's office to see what she had for me.

"First of all, Kathryn, I understand from the Personnel Department that you will be gone for quite a long time and LuAnn will no longer be with us." She pursed her lips and looked down at her desk. "It looks as if we will be short-handed."

"Did LuAnn quit?"

"Not exactly. I took your advice about correlating the thefts with the workstation assignments." She paused dramatically. "It all pointed to LuAnn."

Suddenly I remembered the big tote bag LuAnn carried around. "Of course, she had that big bag. Somehow

111

she got the items out of the lab work area, and then took them from the building in that tote bag."

"Exactly. Three days ago we had security check everyone's packages and bags as they left. We explained it as a routine request from our corporate office. We found four HPLC columns in LuAnn's bag. When we interviewed her, along with the appropriate people present, she broke down and admitted everything."

I noticed Dr. Lan didn't say when "we" interrogated her.

"She told us that her husband met a man in a bar, and when he found out his wife worked in a lab, he offered hundreds of dollars for any analyzer parts and test kits she could get for him."

I came close to feeling sorry for LuAnn, but then she received a good salary here at the lab and her dishonesty had caused Dr. Lan, and myself, a lot of anxiety.

Dr. Lan stood, came around her desk, and walked me to the door, putting her hand on my elbow. "Kathryn, I hope your mother has a rapid recovery. We will miss you." Her voice was a degree warmer than usual.

"Thank you." I wasn't sure what more there was to say. Dr. Lan and I were as close as we would ever be and I now realized the work here had become routine and boring. Then I remembered my assignment for the day. "What about my project?"

"Oh, yes." Dr. Lan glanced back at her desk and randomly picked up some pages from a procedure manual. "Please review these and see if they are up-to-date." She hesitated, and then looked away. "Kathryn, you may leave early today."

As I took the pages I wondered if Dr. Lan knew I was really going to Paris for the agency. If she did, she certainly wasn't going to tell me. As aloof as she had always been, I would miss her.

†

Early that evening I was tidying up my apartment and looking over my not too extensive wardrobe when the phone rang.

"Happy belated New Year."

I hadn't expected to hear from her again. "Kitty, why are you calling me?"

She seemed to be taken aback by my abruptness as she hesitantly replied. "Well, it's the New Year and I was afraid you were upset with me. I don't want that. I don't want to start the year off with trouble between us."

"Kitty, there is nothing between us." I was about to hang up when I thought of a way Kitty might help me. For the past few days, thinking of leaving my apartment empty for six weeks had bothered me. There might be a solution. Could I risk it? "Have you found an apartment?"

"No, and I'm getting worried. I have to be out in less than two weeks."

"The lab is sending me for a training program, and then I'll be staying on to help them train others. I'll be gone at least six weeks." I took a deep breath and plunged ahead. "Maybe you could stay here for a few weeks. But," I used my firmest tone, "you have to be out before I get back."

"Kat, that would be great. And I promise you I will be gone by the time you return home."

I gripped the phone. What had I just done?

"That's a long time, where are you going?" Kitty asked before I could change my mind.

113

I thought quickly. "California." The agency could arrange for postcards to come from me.

"Look, Kat, let's get together, just to say goodbye."

After what happened Christmas Eve I didn't want to risk being alone with her, because I wasn't sure if I could trust myself. Kitty was waiting for an answer. Maybe we could have a brief meeting in a place that was not too intimate. "How about a drink at the place around the corner?"

"I can meet you in an hour," Kitty said eagerly.

"All right." I hung up with the uneasy feeling that Kitty had once again successfully manipulated me.

Kitty and I used to occasionally stop in The Spotlight Lounge in what I now thought of as the old days. I got dressed and walked there, trying to suppress any excitement I felt at seeing Kitty again.

†

Inside, nothing had changed. A long, dark, mahogany bar, facing a pseudo Art Deco mirror, ran along one wall, and booths ran along the other. A few tables took up the center of the room and a television, with the sound turned off, looked down from high in a corner. Faded theater posters on the walls attempted a theatrical theme. This place had regular customers with no attempt to attract the new or trendy trade.

Kitty slid into the booth a few minutes after I arrived. She pulled off her leather gloves, stuffed them in her jacket pocket, and removed her jacket.

"I think I'll have scotch. I'm not in the mood for wine."

As she smiled at me I remembered why I was attracted to her, but I also remembered how she had left me.

"A wise choice. Considering the wine selection here, I'll have one too."

I looked around, remembering all the times we used to come here together. I didn't want to think about them.

A waiter in a white shirt, black, bow tie, and slicked-back hair took our order and then returned with two glasses of scotch and water.

Kitty carefully arranged the napkin under her glass. "I feel badly about everything. You know, Kat; I didn't think you cared that much. You were always so self-sufficient and in your own world."

"I loved you, Kitty." It was a simple statement of how I once felt.

"I didn't see that. When Mary Beth came along I couldn't help myself." Kitty avoided looking at me.

We sat there with our drinks and then Kitty said. "So, you're going to California for the lab. What happened about the thefts?"

After all our time together, I didn't feel right deceiving Kitty about the trip, but I couldn't betray the agency. I had to keep up the story about going to California.

"Dr. Lan correlated the times the equipment disappeared with who was working in that area at the time. It pointed to one of our chemists."

Kitty nodded. "Pretty smart of Dr Lan."

I didn't tell her it was my idea. It didn't really matter now. The lab was behind me. I tried to think of a safe subject. "How are your parents?" As soon as I said this I remembered they lived in southern California. If Kitty suggested I visit them my training would be in San Francisco with no time to travel down there.

"Oh fine. They have their own lives, but I do hear from them now and then." Kitty's look softened. "It must be hard for you with no family. I guess I never realized that."

My hand rested on the table and she reached across and put her fingers on it. "Is there any hope for us to ever get back together again?" I saw she was wearing the bracelet I gave her.

"No, Kitty." I knew that my feelings for her were no longer the same. I was finally ready to move on with my life.

She nodded and withdrew her hand. We sat in silence as we finished our drinks. I signaled for the check, which Kitty insisted on paying. "It's the least I can do." She laid down some bills.

On the sidewalk in front of the bar, Kitty leaned over and lightly kissed my cheek. "Have a safe trip and don't worry about the apartment. I'll take good care of it."

"I leave Tuesday. You can pick up the keys from my neighbor, Pat." I paused. "Goodbye, Kitty."

I left her standing there with a look of confusion on her face as I hurried away. I hadn't asked her how things were with the doctor, but I knew Kitty would never bring her to my apartment.

†

The next day I did some shopping. My taste was fairly conservative. I bought some good slacks, a few sweaters, and a simple black dress in case some important social event came up. My old trench coat had been to the dry cleaners too many times, so I bought a black, cashmere wool, polo coat. I also bought some new underwear.

My last stop was at the bookstore where I met Adriana. When I entered I must have looked lost because a clerk approached me. "Can I help you find something?"

Grateful for her help I told her what I wanted. "I'm looking for a book that describes the different operas, you know, the plot, arias, and history."

"This way." I followed her to the music section, and watched as she put on the glasses hanging on a chain around her neck, and ran her finger along the spines. She pulled out a book. "Here is a good one."

I looked at the Table of Contents. Several pages were devoted to *Don Carlo*. "I'll take this."

That evening I sat down with my opera book and read a description of *Don Carlo* that referred to it as an opera lover's opera that combines wonderful music with a psychologically thrilling, poignant drama. When I read further that every production of *Don Carlo* became a major venture for an opera company, I understood how fortunate it was that her company had Adriana Desi, who knew the role and had a classic Verdi voice. I closed the book and set it aside. I did not buy a recording of *Don Carlo* because I only wanted to hear Elisabetta sung by Adriana Desi.

†

The agency picked up my car on Friday and, after they left, I pulled a briefcase from the back of a closet where it had resided since Kitty moved out over a year ago. I opened it and took out the manuscript of my novel, spreading the pages on the table in front of me.

The story was a mystery involving an evil child who committed several murders over the years. Set in a small town in Wisconsin, it spanned twenty-four years. In the end, the heroine invites the town librarian, an attractive woman, to live with her in her grandparents' large Victorian home, which she has inherited. It would have been more enjoyable to make them lovers, but this was a mainstream novel so I had them move in together for economic reasons.

Reading through it, I had an idea for another chapter where the evil child goes to Girl Scout camp. I vaguely remembered my days as a Girl Scout back in Wisconsin. What I needed was an old Girl Scout Handbook, which I could probably find in a used bookstore. If I was going to be a writer I had to start writing again. I went to my bookshelf and took down an empty notebook I had bought to jot down my ideas for the book. It could go to Paris with me. Looking at the typewritten pages, I realized that I was right when I told Kitty that I would have to get a computer. I straightened the pages and then pushed them back into the briefcase.

The following day I sat down and wrote a note to Valerie Patterson, the flute player I met in Washington, D.C. I explained that I was going on a trip abroad with friends and expected to be gone at least six weeks. I hoped she would get the college position she wanted, and whoever hired her, they would be lucky to get her. I ended by promising to keep in touch. I didn't say it, but hoped she would find her little house and also someone to share it with.

Next I called my neighbor, Pat. She was a widow who lived alone, and I didn't think it would be difficult to find her home. After several rings she picked up sounding out of breath.

"Hi, Pat, it's Kathryn. I hope I'm not disturbing you."

"No, not at all. I was in the other room cleaning out dresser drawers."

"I'm leaving Tuesday for a trip to Paris and a friend is going to stay here in my apartment. Could I leave the keys with you?"

"Paris? How exciting. Of course, let's see. I'll be home Monday afternoon. How about four o'clock? I'm having lunch with friends at noon."

At four on Monday, I walked down the hall to Pat's apartment and rang the bell. After some fiddling with the lock the door flew open.

"Kathryn, come in. Look who's here, Mitzi."

Across the room reclining on a plaid blanket at the end of the couch was Pat's smoky-colored, longhaired cat. Mitzi yawned and regarded me lazily with her round yellow eyes, I crossed the room and gently stroked her silky fur. Looking at Mitzi reminded me of the abandoned cats and dogs the agency found on the White Moon farm. I wondered whatever happened to them. Hopefully, the agency had turned them over to a shelter.

"She doesn't like this weather. No sun shining in the windows, but I keep it nice and warm for her." I saw Pat looking affectionately at Mitzi.

Indeed the apartment was very toasty, and I already regretted wearing my heavy wool ski sweater as a bead of perspiration trickled down my back.

"I was about to have a cup of tea. Will you join me?"

"Yes, that would be nice." At that moment a teakettle began its high-pitched whistling and Pat hurried into the kitchen.

I had a special affection for Pat. She had befriended me last year before Christmas after Kitty moved out. She knew I was alone, and with the holiday season approaching, Pat had invited me to her apartment for Christmas cookies and a glass of wine. It was a gesture I always appreciated.

A few minutes later she carried two ornately decorated cups and saucers into the room. I accepted mine. "These are lovely cups."

"I got them when Tim and I were in England. I hope you like Irish tea, that's all I drink."

The tea was too hot to try. "Oh yes, I'm sure it's good." I recalled earlier references to Tim, evidently the departed husband.

As she settled down next to Mitzi, I noticed Pat's graying brown hair looked freshly permed, probably for the holidays. Across the room sat a tabletop Christmas tree, festively laden with decorations, and a knit stocking with Mitzi's name on it had been pinned to the window curtain. Pat's living room carpeting had recently been vacuumed, leaving lines that resembled the furrows of a plowed field.

"Kathryn, thank you again for the Christmas gift, such a large, lovely box of chocolates. Of course they're all gone. And Mitzi loved her toy." She looked around. "I don't see it, probably under the couch."

Pat took a sip of her tea. "So, you are going to Paris. Not really the best time of the year to be there."

"A friend of mine is going on business and invited me to go along."

"Well, that's different. Do you speak the language?"

"No, but I believe she does. "I gulped my hot tea wanting to change the subject before Pat asked more questions about my friend. "How was your Christmas?" I knew she had gone to Texas to visit her son and his family.

"Just wonderful. Those grandchildren are so much fun, and so smart."

Before I could hear the exploits of the grandchildren, I emptied my teacup and looked at my watch. "I better get going, I have to finish packing. I told Kitty to call you to arrange a time to pick up the keys. One that is convenient for you."

Pat took my cup and saucer. "Kitty? Isn't she the woman that used to live with you?"

"Yes, well she moved away to go to school," I quickly added. "She's back now."

"I see. Anytime is fine. I'm almost always home except for my exercise class and bridge club." She added, "And my book club."

"Thanks again, Pat." At the door I turned back. "Bye, Mitzi." Seeing Mitzi curled up in a tight ball fast asleep I didn't expect a response.

†

Later that night in my apartment with my packing done, my suitcases stood in the living room. I put the Christmas tree away, and returned my novel to the closet. Putting on Adriana's recording, I poured a glass of wine, turned out the lights, and lay back listening to the recording for the last time. My thoughts were of the upcoming trip, the assignment I never wanted, and all those I would be leaving behind: Kitty, Michele, Dr. Lan, Valerie Patterson, and even Pat and Mitzi. Most of all I mourned the loss of my friend, Carmen.

Why was I doing this? Then as I listened to Adriana Desi's voice I knew I wanted to be with her. That was why I was going to Paris.

Chapter Sixteen

Tuesday morning Adriana's manager, Jack, drove us to the airport in his black Mercedes. Maria sat up in front next to him as they carried on an animated discussion of their favorite Italian dishes. I sat in back with Adriana, exhausted after a mostly sleepless night. When I had finally fallen asleep toward dawn, I dreamed of Kitty begging me not to leave her and Michele issuing stern warnings about the dangers of the trip.

I wondered how Adriana felt about flying to Paris to step into a major role on short notice, but when I looked over at her, she appeared calm and happy.

Turning to me she smiled, reached over, and pressed my hand. "Kathryn, I'm so glad you are going with me."

I relaxed and sank into the soft leather of the seat.

After checking in and going through security we walked to our gate. We heard our flight announced and our seating row called. Embraces and kisses descended on Adriana.

Jack shook my hand. "Take good care of Adriana," he ordered.

I even got a brief hug from Maria who added, "Have a safe trip."

Seated in the business class next to Adriana, I fastened my seat belt. The plane taxied down the runway and then rose in the air. The lights were dimmed after drinks and the meal.

Wide awake now, I wanted to hear about the rehearsal schedule ahead for Adriana. "What's going to happen in the next few weeks?"

Adriana arranged her pillow and blanket and leaned back. "For the next three weeks we have studio rehearsals with a piano accompanist, and then the stage rehearsals begin."

"You don't rehearse with the orchestra?"

"Not yet, but separate orchestral and choral rehearsals are taking place with the conductor and chorus master. Two days before opening night we have a dress rehearsal."

All I could think of was what a grueling schedule she faced. I wondered where I would fit in and how I could help her.

Adriana turned toward me. "Kathryn, do you regret this decision, leaving everyone behind to go off with me like this for such a long time?" Her dark eyes were anxious.

I realized she knew nothing about how lonely my personal life was or how I felt about her. "No, I'm really looking forward to this," I said, hoping to put us both at ease.

She reached over and pulled up my blanket. "Try to get some sleep now." She touched my arm and added softly, "We will have a good time."

Despite her reassuring words, I was suddenly apprehensive about going to a strange city with a woman described by Michele as dangerous, even though I knew she was wrong.

I didn't think I could get to sleep, but I must have, because when I opened my eyes the cabin was light, people were moving around, and I could smell the aroma of coffee.

Adriana was watching me and smiling. "You didn't have any trouble sleeping, that's good." She looked rested and fresh.

†

After we landed and cleared customs, a driver met us and drove us to our hotel. Small but elegant, it was a short taxi ride to the opera house, the older Palais Garnier where Adriana would be performing, not the new Opera Bastille. From my reading I learned that the Palais Garnier was an elegant, 1,979-seat opera house, built during the period of 1861 to 1875 for the Paris Opera and famous for the Grand Staircase in the entrance hall of marble. The architectural style was described as Second Empire and Beaux-Arts.

We checked in and went up to our rooms where Adriana had a small suite, and I had a room with an adjoining door. After unpacking we strolled around the neighborhood in the dusk, stopping to look in shop windows.

"Let's have an early dinner here." Adriana pointed to a small, inviting bistro. We went in and a waiter led us to a table.

Everything had happened so rapidly, and now here I was in a foreign city, sitting across from a woman I hardly knew, and trying to read a menu I could barely decipher.

Adriana frowned as she examined her menu. "I don't want anything too heavy." Then she looked up at me and smiled. "What do you think, Kathryn? What looks good to you?"

When I saw her sincere expression and warm smile, any lingering doubts about the trip were gone. I trusted Adriana and knew the agency was wrong about her involvement with the White Moon.

Back at our hotel, I was asleep as soon as I fell onto my bed. That night there were no troubling dreams to disturb me.

†

The next afternoon after lunch, we left the hotel for Adriana's two o'clock rehearsal.

"Are you ready, dear?" Adriana asked.

Looking the part of my role as assistant, I picked up the briefcase containing music and a sweater along with the thermos of tea.

On the way to the rehearsal, sitting together in the taxi, Adriana explained, "I am singing the role of Elisabetta, Elisabeth of Valois, a French princess who was initially betrothed to Don Carlo, but then instead was married to his father, King Phillip. Causing many complications." She laughed and went on, "Verdi originally wrote *Don Carlo as Don Carlos*, a five-act version in French, but this performance will be the shorter, four-act, Italian version of 1884."

"I'm glad you're going to be at the Palais Garnier, not the Opera Bastille. I read there was a lot of controversy and scandal even before the new theater opened in 1989."

"Yes, it was to be the only opera venue of the Paris National Opera, but many of the audience preferred the ornate decoration of the more traditional Palais Garnier to the cold, sterile, modern design of the Opera Bastille." She turned to me smiling. "I am glad they are now also performing operas at the Palais Garnier. I love singing there."

Although we arrived before two o'clock most of the other singers were already there. Walking into the rehearsal room, I had not anticipated the reception given Adriana.

There was applause as everyone surrounded her and seemed genuinely pleased to see her.

"Darling!" A buxom woman with short curly hair ran up to embrace her, and a tall gray-haired man dramatically exclaimed, "Adriana, my dear," as he kissed her hand.

Standing back and watching, I was so happy for her and proud to be with her.

Except for listening to her recording, I had never heard Adriana sing. As the rehearsal proceeded I realized that not only did she have a beautiful voice, but also she was well prepared for her role, and treated her colleagues graciously and professionally. They in turn all seemed truly fond of her.

When the rehearsal ended, Adriana came over and sat down next to me. "Kathryn, would you mind terribly if I sent you back to the hotel alone? You could eat in the restaurant there."

She brushed a lock of hair out of my face. "Andre wants to go over some of the staging with me and then discuss other aspects of the production over dinner. I am already two weeks behind and the stage rehearsals start in three weeks."

Suzanne Zantec, the mezzo singing the role of Princess Eboli, overheard us. "I'll take her back, she can ride with me."

I said goodbye to Adriana and left with Suzanne.

✝

Suzanne had a car waiting for her in front. During the rehearsal I had watched her and decided she was talented, respected by her colleagues, and possessed a no-nonsense, confident attitude. I thought that she was the kind of person who had worked very hard for her career. Physically, she was heavier and not as tall as Adriana, with features that would not be considered immediately attractive, but she had a bright, open smile and friendly manner.

Suzanne settled back in the seat, ran her hand through her short, curly brown hair, and examined me. "I thought I saw you with Adriana last year in London, but now I'm not sure it was you. Was it you? How long have you known Adriana?"

"No, not me. I've only known Adriana a short time. Maria was supposed to come with her, but Sophia broke her hip." So she had seen Nicole with Adriana in London. The trip Maria didn't make.

"Maria's mother? Is she all right?"

Uneasy with Suzanne's reference to Nicole, I kept the talk centered on Maria and Sophia. "Yes, I guess she's going to be fine, but Maria was disappointed she couldn't come to Paris. Sophia has to go to a rehabilitation home."

When we pulled up in front of the hotel, Suzanne leaned forward and looked out the car window. "Do they have a bar?"

"Yes, a small one. I saw it when we checked in."

"Let's have a drink together. I can take a taxi from here." She climbed out of the car and I followed.

We entered the warm, dimly lit bar, and sat at a table together. Suzanne arranged her coat on a chair back, crossed her legs, and leaned back. I almost expected her to take out a cigarette and light it, but knew she was the kind of singer who took special care of her voice. Like Adriana, it was the center of her life.

The drinks arrived, wine for me, some kind of liquor with a splash of something for Suzanne. She took a sip.

"We are all so glad to have Adriana join us. Her predecessor was a nightmare. Demanding, rude, late for rehearsals, and unprepared. Everyone adores Adriana. She's a wonderful colleague and it's great she's singing again. She sounds fabulous." Sighing she added, "I hope I never go through a vocal crisis like hers. I try to keep my engagements and personal life as uncomplicated as I can."

She lifted her glass. "My friend Jeffrey is joining me here as soon as he can. I might as well warn you, he is younger than I am." She added confidentially. "It sometimes causes talk."

I tried to determine her age—late thirties, early forties perhaps. "If it was the other way around and he was much older, no one would think anything of it."

"You are so right." She moved on. "I have an apartment while I'm here; we're staying on another month. I have some recitals scheduled, nothing too taxing."

I wondered about her reference to Adriana's vocal crisis and a singer's personal life. Having a younger lover that caused talk was not exactly keeping Suzanne's life uncomplicated.

We ordered another drink and then Suzanne leaned across the table. "What, if I may ask, do you do that you could take off to come here with Adriana?"

"I'm a chemist. I work in a drug testing lab. The job was becoming routine so I took a leave. I can always go back." With the time change and not eating much for lunch, the second drink was making me feel relaxed and a little detached.

"A scientist, how interesting. Well, I'm glad you came with Adriana. It really helps to have someone with you for support. Maria is devoted to Adriana, but she is older and sometimes a little controlling. I can't wait until Jeffrey gets here." She arranged the napkin under her glass. "By the way, you don't need to have any thoughts that the meetings between Adriana and Andre are anything other than professional. He prefers men, or more particularly the rehearsal pianist. They are an item."

I remembered the pleasant young man with long dark hair at the piano during the rehearsal. Andre, the director, appeared to be in his early fifties, with a neatly trimmed beard showing a little gray.

"I'm sure he's talented, but Andre seemed kind of nervous and excitable at the rehearsal." Fortunately, he appeared to like Adriana.

"Yes. Well, luckily Claude knows how to put everyone at ease. Once he even made Andre laugh."

Suzanne looked at her watch, something fancy with an ornate gold band and the face sprinkled with many jewels. "I better get going after this one, big day tomorrow. Is the restaurant here okay? Can you get something to eat if I leave you?"

"I'm fine. I still have a little jet lag so I'll go to bed early." I could barely keep my eyes open.

She signaled for the check and paid it despite my protests.

"Take care, glad you are here." She patted my arm, put on her coat, and left. As I watched her leave I decided I liked her and was pleased that she was here in Paris performing in *Don Carlo* with Adriana. It would be helpful for Adriana to have a supportive colleague.

Later, back in my room, I got ready for bed and then, propped up with pillows, I opened a new issue of *Time*. I had left my door slightly ajar hoping to hear Adriana when she returned. Just as I was thinking of turning out the light, there was a soft knock on my door.

"Kathryn, are you awake?" Adriana peered in.

"Yes, I am." I eagerly sat up and put the magazine aside. Adriana entered and started toward the chair near the window, but I patted the bed.

As she sat down on the edge she laughed. "Did Suzanne deliver you back safely?"

"She came in and we had a drink together in the bar. I like her."

"I'm glad to hear that. We have appeared together before in several operas. I always look forward to working with her."

I was nervously aware of Adriana on my bed, a few feet away from me. I searched for a subject to keep her there. "How was your dinner and meeting with Andre?"

"I could not eat much. I am still tired from the flight and the time change." She pushed her hair back. "I have never worked with Andre before, but he has an international reputation and his productions are considered conventional and yet powerful. Not controversial reinterpretations. He is a little high-strung, but I know we are going to get along well."

Adriana stifled a yawn and began unbuttoning her blouse. "I had better turn in." She put her hand down on the bed next to me. "And you too," she said with a smile before touching my hand.

"Good night." I watched her leave, wishing she were staying with me.

Chapter Seventeen

Rehearsals, costume fittings, and meetings filled the next days. At the end of a busy day Adriana returned to the hotel too tired to do much more than eat, review the day's events with me, take a bath, and go to bed. But some evenings we bundled up, went out walking in the neighborhood, and ate at the small bistro nearby. When the rehearsals began later in the day, I went out for a run in a nearby park.

One late afternoon, we walked together to an area of boutiques and small shops. As we passed in front of a boutique, Adriana paused. "Let's go in here and look around." She started toward the door.

"Just a second, I want to look at something in the window, I'll be right in." A jacket had caught my attention, and as I peered in the window I saw my reflection, but something more. Another reflection behind mine, which looked like me. I thought with the setting sun it must be a trick with the lighting, but I saw a difference in the other reflection. A grinning face and longer hair. I briefly closed my eyes and when I opened them the reflection had disappeared. I spun around, seeing no one behind me, but merging into the crowd I saw the back of a woman's head with light hair and about my height.

"Did you see something you liked in the window?" Adriana stood beside me.

Still dazed by what I had seen, I shook my head. "No, I was just looking at the crowd."

"I didn't find anything of interest in there, we can go on." Adriana looked at me closely. "Is everything all right, Kathryn?"

"I'm fine." I attempted a smile. "It's just that sometimes I'm overwhelmed, being here in Paris and with you."

"I feel that way myself sometimes. This has all been so sudden. "But," she said warmly, "I am so glad you are here with me."

Sure that the lighting and my overworked imagination had been responsible for seeing the reflection, I put it out of my mind as Adriana took my arm and we walked on.

The next day when we returned to the hotel from the rehearsal, Adriana stopped at the desk to pick up her mail and then, while sorting it in the elevator, announced she had received a letter from Maria.

She looked at the envelope. "I wonder how Sophia is doing?" Sighing, she added, "I'm sure Maria is wishing she could be here in Paris with us."

Wanting to give her some private time alone to read the letter, I went to my room, closed the door, and undressed for bed. I got out the notebook I had brought along to jot down ideas about my novel, and lay down on the bed with it. I opened it up and stared at the blank first page. Too intimidating. I turned to the third page and wrote a few ideas for the Girl Scout camp chapter. I didn't attempt an outline because I never knew what direction the story line might take.

About a half hour later, Adriana knocked softly on my door.

"Kathryn, are you still awake?"

"Yes, come in." Out of ideas, I gladly laid my notebook aside and sat up on the edge of my bed, while Adriana sat in one of the chairs near the window, holding the letter in her hand. I thought how lovely she looked, wearing a white satin robe over pale green, silk pajamas, with her hair down around her shoulders.

Seeing the letter I asked, "How's Sophia doing?"

"She is doing so well that she is going to be leaving the rehabilitation home." She turned over the letter. "Maria wants to take her to Florida."

"Florida?"

"Yes, Renata and Marco have a place there and an apartment is for rent in their complex. They urged Sophia and Maria to come down."

"I'm surprised Sophia would want to go there."

Adriana looked up. "It seems Florida has a certain glamour for the older generation, and it will be good for her to get away from the cold and snow in New York. They just had another big snowfall."

I briefly wondered if Chris and her friends went on their ski trip, and if she had even thought to call me. It seemed so long ago when she invited me, but now I no longer had any interest in it.

Adriana set the letter aside and leaned forward. "You know, Kathryn, we talked about your work, but I never asked if you play a musical instrument."

"I played the flute in grade school and high school. While I was in college I took some recorder lessons and played with an ensemble. Unfortunately, my recorder group in New York broke up just before Christmas." I made a face. "It was very disappointing." I didn't go into any detail about my dysfunctional group.

"An instrument with a long history, the recorder." She looked at me with concern. "Isn't it possible for you find another group to play with?"

"I think when I go back to New York I will see if I can find one. Maybe I'll even learn to play a new instrument, like the baroque flute." I remembered how much I had enjoyed playing with my original group, and smiled at the exciting possibility of a new group and a new instrument.

Adriana returned my smile. "That sounds so interesting. I can tell you enjoy playing and I'm sure you are good." We sat for a moment and then she stretched her arms over her head and yawned. "I'm going to bed. How about you?"

"Yes, I am too." After she left, I turned out the light and lay back, trying to imagine what it would be like having Adriana in my bed next to me.

Chapter Eighteen

Adriana was a different person from the woman I knew in New York.

Back in the opera world with the rehearsals going well, Adriana appeared alive, happy, and confident. The sad, pensive look I had seen so many times in New York had disappeared. If possible, I found her even more attractive.

As for me, I found I thoroughly enjoyed being in Paris with Adriana. I loved the beautiful sights and sounds of the city. Three years ago when I returned to the States from my Peace Corps assignment, I traveled through Europe, but we only spent a few days in Paris. The other volunteers, Jan, Linda, and Kitty, were anxious to get home. I barely remembered our short stay here.

The next morning as we prepared to leave the hotel for a rehearsal, Adriana stopped me before we left her room.

"This sweater," she took the sleeve of my sweater in her fingers, "is it heavy enough? You know that place can be cold in the morning." Adriana was standing very close to me and I held my breath trying to remain calm as my heart pounded.

"It's fine. I'll be all right. I'm supposed to be watching out for you." Why couldn't I think of some clever reply? Nicole probably could have.

Adriana moved her hand down to my bare wrist. "I brought you here; I have to take care of you." She leaned closer and lightly kissed my cheek. I took a deep breath and swallowed trying to regain my composure. She kept her hand there for a moment and then walked away.

Seemingly unaware of her effect on me, Adriana reached the door and then stopped and turned to me.

"Kathryn, you know you don't have to come to all the rehearsals with me. As much as I enjoy having you there, are you sure you wouldn't like to sometimes explore the city instead?"

I looked around for the briefcase. "Not without you." I suspected that when they were in Paris together, Nicole seldom attended the rehearsals with Adriana. I was here to be with Adriana.

Adriana paused and appeared to be thinking. "Kathryn, we have Sunday off, of course, no rehearsal that day. Should we see something of Paris? Perhaps visit a museum? Nothing as grand as the Louvre. There is the Museum d'Orsay, not too far from here, and it is very popular. It just opened two years ago."

"I read about it in a guidebook before we arrived." I recited what I had read. "They have a huge collection of French painters and sculptors from the mid 19th century up until the start of the First World War."

"Yes, many of the famous French Impressionists are there. I think we would like it. Should we go?"

"Let's." I couldn't wait.

†

Early Sunday afternoon we set off on foot for the Museum d'Orsay, wanting to walk as much as we could. The January days were growing gradually longer and the air, though still cold, felt crisp and clean with clear skies.

Adriana appeared very stylish with a long scarf wrapped around her neck and a knit cap on her head to protect her from the cold. Parisians flooded the streets, and because of the low tourism this time of the year, the popular attractions were not so crowded.

As we walked along together Adriana stopped and pointed to a car parked at the curb.

"Look Kathryn, that car is like yours."

A red MGB sat there, older than mine, but in very good condition. I looked it over and peered inside while Adriana watched me.

"Do you miss your car?" She asked with an anxious tone.

I reassured her. "Not right now. It's safely in storage, out of all the snow."

Adriana smiled and nodded. "That's good."

We resumed walking.

Arriving at the square next to the museum we walked around examining six bronze allegorical sculptures set in a row. Adriana put her gloved hand on the sculpture entitled *Oceania*.

"These are so interesting. I have to find out more about them."

As she looked up at the sculpture, I wished I had a camera to take her picture at this moment, she was so lovely standing there. Why hadn't I brought my camera? I had once been so interested in photography and taken many good pictures in Thailand. Photography was something else I gave up when Kitty left me.

An impressive Beaux-Arts building, originally constructed to be a railway station, housed the Museum d'Orsay. Inside, all three levels contained the artwork, but we spent most of our time on the top floor examining the Impressionist collection. I found it interesting that Adriana tended to prefer paintings of people and I liked the landscapes.

Pausing in front of a Renoir painting entitled *Girls at the Piano*, Adriana mused, "I wonder if there is a story behind this painting?"

"I don't know, but even if there is I would rather imagine my own."

Adriana put her arm through mine. "What would it be?"

I cocked my head as I examined the painting. "Two girls enjoying one another's company. And enjoying music."

"Do you think they are sisters?"

"I hope not."

As I stood there in front of the picture close to Adriana, I never wanted this moment to end, but knew it would. We would return to New York, and Maria and Sophia would come back from Florida and move in with Adriana, while I would go on living in my apartment, and probably continue working at the lab. I wondered if Adriana was also thinking about our future as she slowly released my arm.

"Let's go somewhere and have a glass of wine and something to eat."

We were leaving the museum when Adriana glanced into the gift shop. "I would like to stop in here and see if I can get a book about the paintings." She added, "I want something to help me remember this day."

While Adriana looked over the books, I wandered over to look at a display of postcards and posters with reproductions of the artwork. When Adriana came over to me carrying her bag, I pointed to the postcards. "Do you want to send one to Maria?"

Adriana paused and shook her head. "No." She added mischievously, "I would rather have her think I am working hard all the time I am here."

We left the museum laughing together.

Strolling along in the fading daylight, we saw that several of the cafes had well-heated terraces.

"Do you want to sit out there?" Adriana asked.

I shook my head. "No, we better go inside." I didn't want to expose her to any chill. I was there to take care of her and her voice.

With menus and a glass of wine in front of us Adriana glanced briefly at her menu, laid it down and picked up her wine glass. "Kathryn, I am so happy you are here with me. I feel so comfortable with you." She added, "And safe."

I remembered Kitty accusing me of not showing I cared enough. I did not want to make that mistake with Adriana. "I can't think of anywhere I would rather be than right here with you." I wondered if Nicole ever told her that.

"Thank you." Adriana smiled, tilted her head, and looked at me with what I could only describe as affection. "This day has been so enjoyable. I don't want it to end. What do you think, Kathryn, should we have another glass of wine?"

That night lying in bed waiting for sleep to come I wondered what she meant when she said she felt safe with me. Was there someone with whom she hadn't felt safe?

Chapter Nineteen

On a cool, sunny morning, Adriana insisted I go for a run instead of accompanying her to the rehearsal. "Kathryn, I think it will be good for you to get outdoors, and I know you are used to having more exercise." Smiling, she tied the belt of her robe and touched my arm.

"Of course I will miss not having you with me, but today is a shorter rehearsal. I won't be late. Go out and enjoy the day."

After Adriana left I began pulling on my running clothes. In the back of my mind I had a nagging feeling that I had not followed my instructions and contacted the agency on our arrival in Paris. I told myself there was nothing to report. Adriana was here in Paris only to perform in *Don Carlo,* and the agency was wrong about her involvement with the White Moon. I also had an uneasy feeling about Adriana being on her own today without me, despite my instructions to stay with her at all times. But I felt confident she would only go to the rehearsal and then return to the hotel.

As I laced up my running shoes, I reluctantly decided to make a quick call to the agency. I picked up the phone and then set it down. It was such a beautiful day with the sunlight pouring in the window that I didn't want to ruin it by contacting the agency and becoming involved with them. A little more delay wouldn't hurt. I headed for the nearby park.

Although early in the morning, several people were already out walking, and I passed a few other runners, panting and intent on getting their exercise.

Fifty minutes later I stopped to retie a shoelace with my foot up on a bench.

"Kathryn, is that you?"

I turned to see a woman waving and hurrying toward me. I waited as she came up and stopped next to me.

"Linda, what are you doing here?"

"I might ask you the same."

We sat down together on the bench. I hadn't seen Linda since before Kitty and I broke up. I remembered Kitty recently telling me Linda and Jan were no longer together. I looked her over. Linda had always been thin, maybe too thin. She hadn't changed much, except now her hair was a lighter shade of blond, and she wore more makeup. I had never considered her attractive, but she always dressed stylishly and exuded energy and confidence.

"I'm here with my boss for an Infectious Diseases Symposium. I take notes and keep things organized." She loosened the colorful patterned scarf around her neck.

"He must be pretty important to be over here."

"She. Dr. Steffen is a woman, a professor at the University of Pittsburgh. She's here presenting a paper and I'm her assistant. Why are you here? Are you on vacation?"

"No, business. I'm here with a friend who's singing at the Paris Opera."

"The Paris Opera? You must be kidding." She looked at me curiously.

I wondered if Linda's relationship to the professor could be more than an assistant. I didn't have to ask as Linda continued.

"You probably heard Jan and I aren't together anymore. Of course I know about you and Kitty. Dr. Steffen had a partner for a really long time, but she died last year and she doesn't seem to be ready for another relationship." She sighed with disappointment.

Not sure how to respond, I asked, "How long will you be here?"

"We're flying home in the morning. She wants to get back." Linda pulled up the sleeve of her fitted, tan wool coat and glanced at her watch. "The symposium starts at eleven, I'm already late—otherwise we could have coffee or a drink together."

"I shouldn't keep you." I was ready for our visit to end.

"Have you ever been to Pittsburgh?"

"No, I haven't." Why did she ask?

Linda moved closer to me on the bench. "You should come and stay with me sometime. I'll show you around, there's a lot to see." She opened a large, expensive-looking, brown leather handbag, and after fishing around, pulled out a business card, which she extended to me.

"Here, call me. We'll get together." Another look, this time definitely flirtatious. She closed her purse and stood.

I sat there holding her card, baffled by this bizarre encounter. "Have a good flight home. Nice to see you, Linda."

Linda patted my arm. "Sorry, have to run." She peered down at me coyly. "You're looking good. Call me."

I watched her leave and then tore her card into small pieces and dropped them into a trash bin. I left the park, looking forward to being with Adriana.

Chapter Twenty

Anxious words were coming from Adriana's room. Sitting up in bed, I heard what sounded like: "No, don't." As I made my way to her door I looked over at the bedside clock—three in the morning. Worried, I rapped softly on her door and then slowly opened it.

Adriana sat up in bed. "Oh, Kathryn, I am so sorry if I woke you."

I crossed the room and sat on the edge of her bed.

"I had a bad dream, that's all." In the dim light of the room, I saw that her dark hair was falling over her face, and her silk pajama top had come partially unbuttoned. I wanted to take her in my arms, hold her, and say some comforting words. As usual when I was with Adriana, I was at a loss of what to do or say. Instead I tentatively put out my hand, which she took and held tightly. With her other hand she pushed back her hair, straightened her pajama top, and then lay back on the pillows, still holding my hand.

She looked up at me. "I am all right, but will you be able to go back to sleep?"

"Yes, I will. Don't you worry about me." Concerned I waited for her to say something more.

"Would you mind if I asked you to leave your door open a little for the rest of the night?" She squeezed my hand and then released it.

"Of course I can. Good night." I stood, hesitated, and not knowing what else to say, went to my room leaving the door ajar.

As I lay in my bed, I tried to figure out what could have caused Adriana's nightmare. I didn't know anything about her childhood in Trieste as we had never discussed her childhood nor mine. The rehearsals were going well and she seemed so happy now. I didn't want to face it, but she likely had been dreaming about Nicole's death and still missed her terribly. I was a poor substitute.

In the morning Adriana seemed to be her usual self and we didn't mention what had happened during the night.

On our way to the rehearsal, Adriana explained the upcoming schedule. "The studio rehearsals are ending and, with two weeks before opening night, the stage rehearsals are beginning. The cast now has to work with the real sets, props, and costumes, many of them for the first time. We singers have to adjust our voices to the acoustics of the huge auditorium, and our movements to the size of the stage." She paused. "It will be a stressful time for some."

I knew that Adriana with her talent, experience, and love of singing, would easily handle the transition. Then I wondered if this explained her bad dream.

†

That night, after returning from a late rehearsal, we decided to stay in and have dinner in the hotel restaurant. The temperature outside had dropped, and the warm restaurant, with subdued lighting and soft music playing in the background, made for an intimate and restful setting.

Across from me, Adriana ate European style with her fork in her left hand. As I watched her, I thought it certainly appeared to be more efficient than the American style of eating.

I picked up my fork. "I forgot to tell you, the other day when I was running in the park, I met a woman I knew in New York."

Adriana put down her knife and fork. "How nice for you, Kathryn. Are you going to get together, maybe for dinner?"

"No, I really didn't know her very well, and she was flying out the next morning. Besides, she's kind of pushy." I paused dramatically. "Can you imagine? She wanted me to come to Pittsburgh to visit her."

I saw Adriana looked amused. "You can't blame her. I am sure she wanted your company and found you attractive."

I waved this away. "I wasn't interested."

Adriana again looked to me as if she was suppressing a smile, but then changed the subject. "Wasn't Suzanne superb at rehearsal today? Her aria *O don fatale* is guaranteed to bring down the house."

True enough, Suzanne had a voice of exceptional power and range. She would get a tremendous ovation, but the one to bring down the house would be Adriana.

"Don't forget Kathryn, tomorrow evening some of our opera group is going out for dinner together. I think it should be enjoyable and Suzanne tells me Jeffrey will be arriving tonight. She appears to be excited about it."

I switched my fork to my right hand after cutting a piece of chicken. "She told me he is younger than she, and it sometimes causes talk."

Adriana wrinkled her brow. "Really? I don't remember any talk."

"Maybe a little drama," I suggested.

Adriana looked up from her plate and smiled impishly. "Yes, perhaps that's it."

†

The next night our opera group sat at a long table in the back room of a chic, bustling restaurant with its low-beamed ceiling and pseudo-stone-lined walls. Small chandeliers containing simulated candles hung from the ceiling and wine bottles dotted the table. Across the table from me, Adriana sat next to Suzanne and Jeffrey who had arrived the evening before. Thin with light hair and a short trim beard, he had a quiet and serious manner, but Suzanne appeared more animated than I had seen her. Somehow she must have found him entertaining. Once, when he leaned over and said something to her, she burst into peals of laughter. To me it appeared as if he had asked her to pass the bread.

Adriana looked attractive wearing the plum-colored sweater she had worn the night we had dinner together in the Italian restaurant in the East Village, while I wore the same sweater as at Adriana's Christmas open house. Now, it all seemed so long ago.

Seated at the head of the table with the rehearsal pianist on his right, Andre actually looked relaxed, and smiled benevolently now that the rehearsals were going well.

We all listened to Juan Diago, the handsome dark-haired tenor who was singing the role of *Don Carlo*, relate an experience in Madrid when his sword had become entangled.

"I pulled and pulled, but it would not come out of the scabbard for my big fight scene." He gestured dramatically to much laughter from everyone at the table.

Once during the dinner, I looked up from my plate to find Adriana's eyes on me. She raised her wine glass and before it reached her lips she smiled at me and winked. My flush of happiness and desire disappeared when I thought that maybe she was reliving the days with Nicole and still saw her former lover when she looked at me. I wondered what Nicole would have done. Probably winked back, and later when they returned to their hotel room, they would fall on the bed together and have passionate sex.

Depressed at the thought I looked down at my plate and picked at my food. When I looked up Adriana was laughing and talking to the woman seated next to her, a young blonde soprano who sang a minor role in *Don Carlo*. I thought Adriana must have loved Nicole very much to give up singing for so many months after her death. Watching Adriana, I knew I was falling in love with her, but my role would always be that of a companion. I would accompany her to the rehearsals and provide company for her meals. But I could never take Nicole's place.

The dinner ended, chairs scraped back, people stood talking and laughing together, while Adriana came over and took my arm, leaning over to be heard above the noise.

"Andre wants me to stay and go over some staging details with him. It will take no more than an hour. Do you want to wait with me or go back to the hotel?"

I didn't want to hang around and be in the way, it would be better to be there waiting for her when she returned to the hotel. "I'll go back, I can take a taxi. The streets are full of them."

"Unless you are tired, wait up for me, I won't be that long." She pressed my arm.

As I left the restaurant I knew I should have contacted the agency and met with them long ago, but the thought of my assignment depressed me and I knew my heart was no longer in it—if it had ever been. Even though I left Adriana alone again tonight, I felt confident it would be only for a short meeting with Andre.

Back at the hotel, I peered into the bar and thought about another glass of wine, but seeing a crowd I went up to my room, leaving the door slightly ajar so I could hear when Adriana returned. I undressed and then got out my notebook. The chapter moved along, but there were several details concerning merit badges that would take some research when I got back to New York and bought an old Girl Scout Handbook. I worked for an hour and then, not able to concentrate any longer, I set it aside.

My guilty feelings about not contacting the agency returned. They were paying my salary and had sent me here to Paris, although I was convinced it was a useless assignment. I would call, just to check in. I got the cassoulet recipe from a book where I used it as a bookmark, figured out the phone number for the agency, and dialed. A woman answered, I recited the prearranged code, and after a wait she transferred me to someone at the agency named Bill.

"Kathryn, we expected to hear from you when you arrived in Paris. Where in the world have you been?" he asked angrily.

I tried to defend myself. "I haven't had any time away from Adriana, and besides, it would have been suspicious to leave her and go off alone somewhere." I continued pressing my case. "I know she hasn't contacted or seen anyone outside the opera cast. There is really nothing to report, I'm convinced she is not involved with that group."

"Kathryn, that is not for you to decide." I heard Bill trying to suppress what I thought was anger.

My first contact with the agency in Paris, and I had already managed to annoy them. To put it mildly.

"We expect to see you here within the next two days and then we'll discuss your further instructions for this assignment. Is that understood?" When I didn't reply he asked. "Did you hear me?"

"I'll try to arrange something." I hung up with a twinge of guilt as it occurred to me that twice Adriana had been at meetings with Andre. What if the meetings were not really with Andre, but with the White Moon members? I quickly dismissed the thought as impossible.

I picked up a magazine and had just started to page through it when I heard sounds coming from Adriana's suite. I knocked on the partly ajar door.

"Come in." Adriana had changed to her robe and seemed preoccupied as she searched through one of her dresser drawers, her back to me. Finally she turned around. "I think I'll have a bath and go to bed." As she talked she looked around the room avoiding eye contact with me. "Did you have a good time tonight? Enough to eat?" She asked absently.

I expected we would sit together talking and laughing over the events of the dinner party. Instead, I stood there awkwardly. "Yes, I had a good time. Did the meeting go all right?" Perhaps there had been some trouble with Andre. "The meeting? Oh, of course, no problems, it didn't take long. I'm really tired. Good night, Kathryn," she said dismissing me.

"Let me know if you need anything." I waited and then added, "See you in the morning."

Confused, I retreated to my room and closed the door. What had caused Adriana to act so strangely? What had gone wrong tonight? I didn't know, and while trying to puzzle it out, I fell asleep.

Chapter Twenty-one

I awoke with the eerie feeling of not being alone. I turned over and sat up with a start. In the faint light of dawn filtering through the curtains, I saw Adriana sitting in the armchair next to the window. Her body was still, her hands resting in her lap.

"What's wrong? Did something happen?" I tried to clear my head of the sleep still enveloping me.

Adriana turned her head toward me.

"Who are you really? Have you been spying on me?" She didn't look angry, just bewildered.

I put my feet down on the floor and sat for a moment, trying to understand what had happened. Then it occurred to me what this was all about—the telephone conversation last night with the agency. Adriana must have returned to her room early and overheard me talking to them.

I had to make a decision, loyalty to the agency or to Adriana. I got up, went over, and sat in the chair opposite her. I shivered, wishing I had put on my robe and slippers in the cold room.

With my heart pounding, I took a deep breath. "My name is Kathryn Austin and I work for a government agency which assigned me to meet and become close to you. They suspect you of being the leader of a group of women terrorists known as the White Moon. There were bombings in London and Paris when you appeared in operas there. Nicole Chapman, a known member of the White Moon, lived on a farm in upstate New York with other White Moon members. The agency thinks you recruited her. You are considered dangerous."

I had done it. I had betrayed the agency because I believed in Adriana's innocence. Nicole may have been a member of the White Moon, but not Adriana.

Adriana appeared stunned. "I cannot understand this. A terrorist group? I know nothing about this. I am an opera singer and that is all." She slowly shook her head.

I hugged my arms around me and waited.

"Nicole a member?" She paused. "It is possible." She ran her hand through her hair. "There were times she disappeared, sometimes for days. It caused trouble between us. I was concerned for her and was afraid something was wrong. She accused me of interfering with her life and trying to control her."

Adriana looked away. "I met Nicole during a vulnerable time of my life. My dear mother had recently died and I never had a serious relationship with anyone. I was always too busy with my career. In the beginning, Nicole charmed and fascinated me."

Unable to believe what I heard, I asked, "In the beginning? Did something change?"

"Nicole became another person, or perhaps she became who she always was. I am not sure. I don't think I really knew her at all. At first I blamed myself for being too possessive. As I said, she would disappear for days, and become angry if I wanted to know where she had been. Then, if I became upset, she would be charming again and I would forgive her." She looked out the window. "This is embarrassing, but I think she used sex as a reward or withheld it as punishment."

I listened in disbelief. Their relationship had not been a wonderful affair cut short by a tragic accident.

"This was all starting to disturb me, not my singing yet, but I was nervous, preoccupied, couldn't concentrate. One night, Nicole came in late, she had been gone for days. I had a performance the next evening and was anxious about her. She had been drinking and we had words, she became angry and slapped me. She was immediately contrite, apologized, and begged me to forgive her. The next day before the performance, she gave me a present, a gold locket, and then talked about the vacation trip we planned to take in the summer." She lowered her voice. "It was too late. I had decided to end the relationship. Something left my heart after she struck me. She frightened me and I was determined not to continue the relationship and have my career affected."

I sat there confused and speechless. Nicole, the woman I thought I could never replace, had been a cruel fraud. How could she have treated Adriana like that?

Adriana passed her hand over her face. "The next day Nicole was killed in the car accident and I had these horrible guilt feelings. Maybe I could have done things differently. Maybe I was at fault. I couldn't perform at all. When I met you, I was recovering and preparing to return to singing. It shocked and scared me how much you looked like Nicole, but in a short time of knowing you I could see you were not like her. I trusted you and I..."

I interrupted. "Please trust me now. I have betrayed the agency by telling you of my assignment, but I believe you are innocent and I am going to find the proof."

I searched desperately for some way to help her. I remembered something I read at the agency in the folder of White Moon information. "Did Nicole have a tattoo?"

"Why yes. Here." She placed her hand on her upper left thigh. "She told me she got it in college. Her friends all had a rose, but she wanted something different...a crescent moon." Adriana paused. "It was really for that terrorist group, wasn't it?"

"Yes it was." I thought for a moment. "Nicole was coming from the farm when she had the accident. We know she was a member of the White Moon and somehow she is still our link to them. Do you remember any of her friends, or places she frequented when you were here with her?"

Adriana frowned and looked down at the carpet. "Yes, once when we went for dinner, to a restaurant here in Paris, she went into the bar and talked to some women. She never introduced me to them. Later, when I asked how she knew them, she said she sometimes came there for a drink when I was rehearsing or performing. She said she liked to have fun with people her own age." She closed her eyes. "That hurt me."

I reached out and took her hands in mine. "Do you remember the place? Could you find it again?"

"Yes. It wasn't far from here. It's within walking distance. I don't remember the name. Perhaps it was *Chez* something."

157

"Tonight we will go there for dinner. Could you recognize any of the women Nicole talked to?"

"I think I could, one especially. I thought she was a mean-looking woman." Adriana shook her head and murmured, "Kathryn, how you must have mistrusted me."

"No." I couldn't let her think that. "I knew all along that the agency was wrong."

"Then you do believe I'm not involved with this White Moon group?" Her expression was one of hope.

"Yes, I do, and please believe that what was an assignment for me is no more. Together we are going to prove your innocence."

She leaned forward. "Thank you, Kathryn."

I tried to think, to formulate a plan. "The locket, do you have it with you?"

She thought for a moment. "I think it is with my jewelry, I never wore it. Do you want to see it?"

"Yes, I would." I released her hands and waited until she returned with a small box. She handed it to me and I opened it to see a plain, gold locket, engraved with a little design of flowers. "May I borrow this, just for a few days?" I wasn't sure why, but somehow I knew that this represented a connection to Nicole.

"Of course, take it." I snapped the box shut and set it aside on the table.

Adriana looked out the window at the growing daylight, then back to me. "I think everything has been said, Kathryn." She rose, hesitated and then turned back, smiling. "It's too late to go back to sleep. Should we have an early breakfast together in my room?"

I returned her smile. "Good idea, order what you like. You know me, I'll eat anything."

Laughing, she went to her room to call for our breakfast order. I sat, looking out at the rising sun, reflecting on how our honesty with one another had brought us closer.

Chapter Twenty-two

We returned from the rehearsal in the early evening. Adriana tossed her things on a chair.

"I didn't expect we would be gone so long. Those costume fittings are always tiring and the place was cold today. Would you mind if I took a quick shower to warm up before dinner?"

"Of course not, go ahead. We don't want to get to the restaurant too early."

While I waited for her in her room, I went to the window, pulled the curtains aside, and looked out. Thinking of our plans for the evening, I worried that we should have made a reservation for dinner, but since Adriana couldn't remember the name of the restaurant, how could we? If we didn't have dinner we could at least have a drink. I continued to look out the window thinking about the night ahead of us and wondering if the woman would show up.

Fifteen minutes later Adriana entered the room tying the belt to her robe. "What are you looking at?" She came over and put her hand on my shoulder.

"I think it's going to rain." I had read in my guidebook that although heavy rains were less common in January, Paris had erratic and sudden downpours.

"Take along that big umbrella you bought in that small shop the other day." She sat down at her dressing table. "Tonight I am wearing the lovely amber earrings you gave me for Christmas" She put them on and then turned to me. "Can you fasten this necklace for me, dear?"

I took the thin silver chain holding the amber pendant, gently pushed aside her damp hair, and bent down wanting to kiss the nape of her neck. Instead, I fastened the clasp and stepped back. Our eyes met in the mirror and I stood there until Adriana broke the silence. "Thank you, Kathryn." She paused. "I'll get dressed in a hurry."

†

We walked the short distance to the restaurant. "There it is." Adriana pointed to the sign, which read *Chez Simone*.

We entered and were lucky when the maitre d' showed us to a table. I reminded Adriana to sit on the side where she had a view of the entrance and could watch for anyone she might recognize. At the height of the dinner hour the place had become crowded. Through a doorway I could see the bar and most of the patrons who were sitting there.

Tonight, looking exquisite, Adriana wore black slacks and a short, dark-green, wool jacket over a white silk shirt, cut low in the front, emphasizing her breasts. Proud to be with her, I glanced around at the other women in the restaurant. All of them were overdressed, overweight, too thin, or had bored faces. I thought that not one of them had Adriana's intelligent expression. None of them had her talent.

Adriana pointed to the wine list. "Kathryn, I know you prefer white wine, perhaps a nice chardonnay. This is one I have had before. I think you will like it."

"Yes, please order it." I replied, relieved of not having to make the decision.

The bottle of wine arrived and Adriana swirled some in her glass and tasted it. She poured some for me. "What do you think, Kathryn?"

I took a drink. "Great. Good selection." I would have loved anything she ordered.

We picked up our menus and Adriana examined hers. "How about this?" She translated. "Diver sea scallops with spaghetti squash and pistachio sauce."

I looked up from my menu, discouraged at trying to translate it, wishing I had studied French instead of German. "I'll have that too."

We sipped our wine and I motioned toward the bar. "Can you see who is in there?"

I watched Adriana strain to look in that direction. "Not very well, but if I remember the women's room is in the back through the bar. Maybe I should make a trip there to have a look."

She left the table and, as I surveyed the room, I realized it would be awkward if anyone who had ever known Nicole saw me. Would they think Nicole had returned from the dead? But in the dim restaurant with my back to the room, I would just hope it didn't happen.

Adriana returned to the table and I couldn't help smiling broadly as she sat down across from me. Maybe I looked foolish, but I was so happy to be with her.

Adriana picked up her wine glass. "I didn't recognize anyone, although there are some people about Nicole's age down at the end of the bar."

I had to ask. "Do you still see Nicole when you look at me?"

"No. There is a difference." She smiled playfully. "You are sexier."

"Me?" I asked in surprise. "I don't think so."

"Your eyes are sexy. Bedroom eyes I think they call them." She tilted her head and grinned. "They are lighter than Nicole's. Yours are truly blue."

"Was Nicole sexy?"

She contracted her eyebrows. "Oh, if it suited her. Often, though, her expression was calculating. She never wanted to talk about her past, but little things made me think she had a good education and a privileged upbringing."

Enough of my asking her about Nicole, I thought, and changed the subject. "I love the way you say my name." With her accent it was something like "Kotryn."

"Oh? I don't say it correctly?" She leaned forward looking concerned. "Tell me how."

"No, don't ever change the way you say it."

"Do you have a, what is it, a nickname?"

"I don't." I never wanted to hear *Kat*, Kitty's name for me. It was something in the past, over and done with. We finished our meal and still no one appeared that looked familiar to Adriana.

"I guess she isn't coming here tonight. Should we leave?" Adriana looked at her watch. "It is getting late. Yes, it's best we go." I could sense the disappointment in her voice.

Outside the restaurant a light rain fell. "Let's take a taxi." I didn't want Adriana getting wet and catching a cold.

"We have your umbrella and it is not too far."

I opened it up and she took my arm, leaning close to me. As we walked I could feel the welcome pressure of her body against mine. When we reached the corner, the rain came down more heavily, and we ducked into a large, deep doorway where Adriana put her arm around me to pull me out of the rain.

After a few minutes she turned to me. "The rain has stopped. Let us get back."

We were so close I could feel her warm breath on my cheek. My heart was pounding as I longed to take her in my arms, hold her, kiss her, and tell her how much I cared for her. But, huddled in a doorway under an umbrella in the rain wasn't the time or place. She deserved better and I didn't have the courage.

Our shoes splashed through the puddles of rainwater as we hurried back to the hotel. I was anxious to get Adriana out of the rain and change our damp clothes before she caught a cold.

†

In my room after I had changed I sat on the edge of the bed reviewing the evening when I heard a soft knock on my door. Eagerly I called out, "Come in."

Adriana, wearing her satin robe and with her hair down, crossed the room and sat next to me on my bed. She had never looked lovelier.

"I want you to know I had such an enjoyable evening, even though that woman did not appear." Although she smiled I could sense the disappointment in her voice.

"I enjoyed the evening too, and don't worry, we'll find her." This said with a confidence I didn't feel.

Adriana stood, put her hand on my shoulder, leaned over and lightly kissed my cheek. "Good night, sleep well."

She left and I lay back wondering if I could ever get to sleep now.

✝

The next morning a heavy rain fell as we left the hotel for the rehearsal. With opening night approaching, the long and intense rehearsal caused a few tempers to flare, but not Adriana's, she always remained the professional. When the rehearsal finally ended and we were preparing to leave, Suzanne approached us with Jeffrey in tow.

"I suppose you two have a night on the town planned." Laughing, she added, "Neither Jeffrey nor I speak French very well and you know how the French are if you can't speak their language perfectly." She nodded at Adriana. "As you do. We've had some comical times."

We stood there waiting for her to elaborate about those times. Instead, she suggested. "We should get together and go out some night, the four of us...that is when we don't have an early rehearsal the next day."

I didn't say anything and Adriana murmured. "Yes, but I'm not sure when that will be."

When we returned to our hotel in the growing darkness the rain fell even harder.

In her room Adriana took off her damp coat and hung it up before turning to me. "You know, Kathryn, I just don't feel like going out anywhere. What about you?"

"Neither do I. I'm not sure I even want to go down to the restaurant."

"Exactly my thought. Let's eat in our room tonight." Adriana walked to the table, picked up the room service menu, and examined it. "Let's have a pot of hot tea with our meal, and how about a decadent dessert like dark chocolate mousse?"

"Sounds great to me." Adriana always knew what to order.

When the food, a Nicoise salad and our dessert arrived, we turned the lights down, opened the curtains, and sat across from each other at the small table in Adriana's room, eating and watching the rain run down the windows, blurring the light from the streetlamps, turning the scene into an Impressionist painting.

Adriana picked up her teacup and took a tiny sip. "It's still hot, just right for a night like this."

She took another sip. "I wasn't sure what to say to Suzanne when she suggested we go out together. I don't know where the four of us would go or what we would talk about."

I poured more tea. "Well, you and Suzanne could talk about opera, and Jeffrey and I could discuss the stock market." It turned out that Jeffrey earned his living as a stockbroker.

Adriana laughed and playfully slapped my hand that was resting on the table. "I am afraid that if she brings it up again we may have to go." Then her tone became serious. "Kathryn, what if that woman does not go to the bar anymore? Or what if she is not even in Paris? That was over a year ago when I saw her at the restaurant."

I already wondered the same thing, but wanted to remain hopeful that she might show up. She was our only link to the White Moon and proving the agency wrong.

"We were there just one night. We can't give up yet."

"Shall we go back there tomorrow?"

"Yes, let's." I added, "And the food was good."

"Kathryn, you do believe that I am innocent and had nothing to do with that group of terrorists don't you?" she asked anxiously.

"Yes, and do you trust me that I am going to prove your innocence?"

"Yes, dear, I do."

†

The next morning when I woke up I went to her room. Adriana had pulled back the curtain and stood looking out the window. She turned around and smiled.

"Good morning, Kathryn. The rain has stopped and it looks like a nice day."

I joined her at the window. "Would you mind if I don't go to the rehearsal with you today? I want to visit the agency. I have an idea about something I want them to check for me." I didn't add that my two days to report to them were up, and if I didn't appear they might come looking for me.

"Of course, I will see you after the rehearsal." She crossed the room and waved to me from the doorway.

I called after her. "You have a dinner date tonight, don't forget."

She turned back laughing. "I won't forget."

†

Early that afternoon I took a taxi to the agency which posed as a travel bureau in a rundown building on an out-of-the-way lane. Faded travel posters blocked the view through dirty windows. Inside, the same type of bored, nondescript clerk as the one in New York sat reading a magazine behind a high counter. This place offered neither bargain airfares nor tours to exotic places. No one would be making his or her travel arrangements here.

I showed my identification to the clerk and then recited the pre-arranged line from the cassoulet recipe for further identification. The clerk yawned, put down her magazine, and stood, showing me to be an unwelcome interruption to her reading.

"We can help you in one of our travel counselor's offices."

She led the way through a door and down a dingy hallway into another room. Inside, I saw a similar but smaller operation than the one in New York. Four men and a woman were in the room, some working intently at computer terminals, others talking on phones, or conferring together as the sounds of clattering printers and ringing phones filled the air.

Bill, the man I had spoken with on the phone two nights before, shook my hand and led me to his small, corner cubicle. Tall with thinning sandy hair and wire rim glasses, he gestured for me to sit down across from him at his desk. As he looked me over I waited apprehensively, expecting a reprimand for not showing up sooner.

"Well, Kathryn, at last we meet. Like you, I'm an American." He leaned back in his chair. "I've been here in Paris for five years with the agency. Great city, Paris." His manner then changed abruptly and he curtly asked "Have you seen the papers today?"

"No, why?"

He reached down to the floor next to him and threw a French language newspaper on the desk, pointed to an article and translated.

"Early this morning at the rush hour a bomb exploded in a Paris Metro entrance. One person was killed and three severely injured. It was an unsophisticated device, filled with nails. Later, a call to a local newspaper identified it as the work of the United Satellites. A statement from the police confirms that they are vigorously investigating and expect to soon identify and apprehend those responsible for this assault on the public."

He pushed the paper aside. "The White Moon is part of this United Satellites, a loose affiliation of different terrorists groups who work together, when they aren't fighting among themselves."

I thought of Adriana's meeting with Andre two nights before. She had only been gone a short time, and if necessary, Andre could confirm that the meeting between them took place. I trusted her. Adriana had no part in this bombing.

I removed the box with the locket from my pocket and laid it on Bill's desk. "Could you have this locket checked for fingerprints? It belongs to Adriana Desi and may have come from a White Moon member. You might find Adriana's prints if she is on file and those of Nicole Chapman. I'm really interested in any others you may find." I wondered if maybe someone else from the White Moon had handled it before Nicole gave it to Adriana. I thought of it as a desperate long shot.

169

Silently, Bill took the box, put it in a plastic bag, zipped it shut, and wrote out a label for it.

"One more thing, I would like a weapon."

Frowning, he grudgingly admitted, "Well, I do have authorization for you to have one. Wait here."

He disappeared into another room and then returned, carrying a package which he set down heavily on the desk in front of me. "Where is Desi now?"

I picked up the package. "At a rehearsal."

Bill leaned forward in his chair. "Kathryn, I don't feel comfortable with giving you a gun. You've already ignored your instructions to report to us immediately on arriving in Paris, and it is not for you to decide whether or not Desi is involved with the White Moon."

I couldn't think of a reply in my defense, so I sat there in silence until Bill finally got up and walked to the door with me.

"You better get back, don't let her out of your sight, go everywhere with her. We expect a report within the week." He paused. "And be careful."

Chapter Twenty-three

Adriana and I sat in *Chez Simone* in nearly the same location as our previous visit. This time we had made a reservation, and Adriana again positioned herself to see the entrance and monitor who came into the restaurant.

Adriana looked elegant in a black wool, knit top, which revealed her splendid body. When I removed my coat she looked me over.

"That blue cashmere sweater is so attractive, the color is perfect with your light hair and eyes." She leaned toward me and softly added, "My lovely Kathryn."

Since I had learned the truth about her relationship with Adriana I no longer felt any competition with Nicole. Even though she was dead, I despised her for the cruel way she had treated Adriana.

Adriana started to pick up the wine list. "Should we have the same Chardonnay as last time? You liked it didn't you?"

"Very much. Yes, please order it," I replied, proud of her knowledge of wine and food.

When our wine arrived, Adriana lifted her glass. "To our finding one another."

I raised mine and lightly touched it to hers. We drank and she set her glass down. Our eyes met and she smiled as she opened her menu.

"The meal I had last time was very good, but tonight I would like to try something different." She frowned as she examined the menu.

I pointed to an item on my menu and pronounced it as best I could. "*Filet de Dorade en Papillotte au Vin Blanc et Julienne de Legumes*. What is this? I can figure out the white wine and vegetables."

Adriana looked up from her menu. "*Dorade* is a small fish from the Mediterranean Sea. Very tasty. You are right about the wine and vegetables. It comes in parchment with a white wine sauce and julienne vegetables." She smiled at me. "I think you will like it."

We closed our menus and Adriana looked toward the bar. "After we order I should make a visit to the women's room to see who is in the bar."

The waiter approached us and Adriana placed our order. After he left, she stood and smiled down at me. "I'll be back shortly."

A few minutes later I saw Adriana crossing the room to our table. Several men in the dining room looked up from their plates and their companions to watch her progress with admiration, probably wondering what lucky man was with her. Oblivious of their attention, she sat down and picked up her napkin. I wondered how they felt when the lucky person turned out to be a blonde American woman.

"I didn't bother with the women's room. The bar is crowded but I looked around as if searching for a friend. She isn't there."

I looked at my watch. "It's early."

What if she didn't show up tonight? Our remaining nights in Paris would be spent haunting this place and being disappointed with each visit when we didn't see her. I tried to change the subject.

"So, the rehearsal went well today?"

Adriana's expression brightened. "Yes, everyone is doing superbly and is now comfortable with performing on the stage. Andre and the conductor both appear pleased." She leaned forward and asked anxiously. "Was everything all right at the agency?"

"I was a little overdue to check in with them, but otherwise it was just a routine meeting." After all the deception I was relieved that I no longer had to lie to Adriana about my association with the agency or my assignment.

I leaned back as our food arrived. Once my plate was in front of me I cut my fish, put the knife down, and transferred my fork to my right hand. "Maybe I should learn to eat European style, it looks more efficient."

Adriana looked up surprised. "Oh, it is just how I learned to eat growing up." Then she smiled warmly. "Don't change. I think your way is charming. Especially in your hands."

I grinned, thrilled and excited to think she was flirting with me. All during our meal I surreptitiously glanced at her until she caught me. I could feel my face heat up, and when she winked at me, I blushed even more.

173

We finished our meal and I looked around. People still entered the restaurant. "It's not late, let's have some coffee, and just stall a little. Otherwise we can come back another night."

"Good idea, Kathryn." Adriana signaled to the waiter. With my lack of French, I let her handle our dealings with waiters, taxi drivers, and shop clerks.

Neither of us wanted coffee, but as I moved my cup around on the saucer, Adriana's body stiffened and she looked down at the table.

"Coming in right now. I know she is the one I saw with Nicole."

I pushed my napkin off my lap and then bent down to pick it up while looking over at the doorway. I saw the back of someone in a short, black-leather jacket.

"I think it's my turn to visit the woman's room. Be right back."

As I walked past the end of the bar I put my head down, coughing and covering much of my lower face with my hand. The last thing I wanted to happen was for someone to see me as the person they might have known as Nicole.

The woman Adriana pointed out stood at the end of the bar ordering a drink. On the wall just outside the women's room hung a huge poster advertising *Absinthe Ducros Fils*. It depicted a woman, wearing an orange, turn-of-the-century dress and a huge matching hat, gleefully holding up a bottle. I stopped to look at the poster with my back to the bar. As I stood there the woman passed me and pulled open the door to the women's room. The light from inside shone on her face, giving me a brief, clear look. She had dark hair, cut short in no particular style, and a defiant, belligerent expression on her face. It was what Adriana had described—a mean-looking face. I would not forget her. Just before the door closed the woman looked back and I quickly turned around hoping she hadn't seen me.

I returned to the table. "I saw her." I looked around, suddenly suspicious of everyone around me. "I think that's enough for tonight."

Adriana nodded and reached for the check.

As we walked back to the hotel in the dark, cold, clear night, Adriana took my arm. My thoughts now focused on the woman who, I felt, was our link to Nicole. Somehow, I had to use her. As we walked on in silence, I sensed that it had upset Adriana to see this woman from her unhappy past.

After a pause she asked, "Kathryn, I don't like to bring this up, but now that we have seen that woman whom we think is a White Moon member, what will we do?"

"I guess I'll follow her and see if she leads me to the others. Maybe I can find out if they have a headquarters somewhere." I planned to return to the restaurant again and find the woman. "I remember you told me that Nicole hung around there while you rehearsed. That might be a good time for me to go there."

Adriana stopped and tightly gripped my arm. "I don't want you to do that. I am sure she is dangerous. Do you think you could tell your agency about her?"

I didn't want to explain that my credibility with the agency was now nonexistent, or that they still believed she was involved with the White Moon. "No, I don't trust them."

"I understand. But, promise me you won't do anything unless we discuss it together first."

"I promise." I would have promised her anything.

We walked on.

†

When we reached the hotel I went to my room, hung up my coat, and changed into my pajamas before I crossed to Adriana's room. I hesitated in the doorway.

She was in her robe standing next to her bed looking at me with a half-smile on her face. "Come over here."

I approached her and she put her hand on my arm, pulling me closer and whispering, "I want you, Kathryn."

I could barely reply. "Oh, Adriana," I stammered, "I want you too."

She put her arms around me, drawing my mouth to hers. We kissed slowly and tenderly. I moved my lips down to lightly kiss her throat. She placed her hands in my hair bringing my lips closer.

I found the belt to her robe and untied it, she removed her arms, and the robe fell to the floor. She was wearing silk pajamas and I carefully began to unbutton the top. She reached up and finished unbuttoning it, and it fell to the floor along with the bottoms. I pulled off my pajama pants and cast the top aside. As we embraced we fell back onto Adriana's bed. I inhaled her scent as I felt the warmth of her body against mine. I kissed her again, more urgently this time. My mouth trailed down to her lovely, full breasts, and she trembled and held me tightly as my tongue lightly brushed her nipples. With my hand between her legs, I stroked the inside of her thigh and shakily whispered, "Do you want me to…?"

She closed her eyes with her head thrown back. "Oh, Kathryn, yes."

I moved my hand up to gently explore her with my fingertips as her body stiffened and she sighed, burying her hands in my hair and drawing my mouth to hers.

Instead of finding a sophisticated, experienced lover, I found a woman desperate for love and unsure if she would receive it. Nicole had used making love as power when it suited her purpose, and withheld it from Adriana when she wanted to hurt her. I would never do that to her.

She gently placed the palm of her hand on my cheek. "Show me more, dear."

I held her shoulders and moved her against the length of my body. "Your turn, my darling." Nicole may not have permitted it, but our lovemaking would be equal.

Her hair brushed my breasts as she leaned over me and tentatively, gently, moved her hands over my body while she explored making love to me. My body responded and I gasped with pleasure, unable to believe that Adriana and I were at last together.

✝

The next morning I awoke to sunlight pouring through the curtains. I sat up abruptly and looked around, realizing I was in Adriana's room. The place next to me was empty.

"Good morning, darling." Adriana came into the room fully dressed and fastening her wristwatch.

"What time is it? We have a rehearsal this morning?" I looked around frantically and stretched to see the bedside clock.

"Don't worry about that, I can go alone today. I have a costume fitting, but it won't take as long as yesterday." She came over to the bed and smiled down at me. "I didn't want to wake you." Sitting on the edge of the bed she put her hand on my arm. "Take your time, go for a run if you like, and let's stay in again together tonight. I don't want to share you with anyone."

"That sounds wonderful, but are you sure about the rehearsal? I can get ready quickly."

"No, it really is all right." She looked at her watch. "For once I wish I didn't have a rehearsal." She sighed. "I better get going and catch a taxi. See you later, enjoy the day." She put her arms around me and we kissed deeply and tenderly. Then she left.

I lay back on the bed, but now, wide awake, I couldn't sleep any longer. It was too early to go back to the restaurant and look for the White Moon woman, and besides, I had promised Adriana not to do anything unless we discussed it first. Maybe a run would be a good idea. I could go to the park a few blocks away where I met Linda. I got up, looked out the window to get an idea of the temperature, and got dressed in my running clothes.

I ran longer than usual. It was a cool but sunny day, and I didn't want to go back indoors yet as my thoughts lingered on the details of the passionate night before.

After my run and back in my room, I undressed and prepared to take a shower when the phone rang. I grabbed a towel, hurried over, and picked up the phone.

"Is Adriana there? This is Andre. We have a rehearsal this morning. I've been trying to call." He continued in his heavily accented English. "Where is she?"

"What do you mean she isn't there? She left in plenty of time. She took a taxi." I looked at the bedside clock. The rehearsal would have started almost two hours ago. Had I heard Andre correctly? How could this be?

"No, she is not here." He paused. "Would something have happened? An accident? Was she feeling well when she left?"

Confused and upset I replied, "I don't know. Andre, please call me if she shows up. Meanwhile, I'll try to locate her."

I hung up and sat down to think. Too much time had elapsed since Adriana left the hotel for the rehearsal. What if she became ill in the taxi or there was an accident and she was in a hospital? The city was full of hospitals and there wasn't any way I would be able to find her in one of them. I knew I was helpless to locate her alone.

Reluctantly, I reached for the phone and called the agency. Someone transferred me to Bill who listened to my panicked explanation of Adriana's disappearance.

"We'll alert the special police force we work with and try to locate the taxi. You had better come down here right away."

I took a quick shower, threw on some clothes, and got there within the hour.

✝

As Bill led me to his desk, I stopped him and asked, "Do you have a picture of Adriana to help the police locate her?"

"Of course we do," he replied testily.

Why wouldn't they? How dumb of me. There would be a complete file on her.

Bill sat down and reached for some papers on his desk before picking up one. "Those fingerprints on the locket. One set was Desi. She was fingerprinted some years ago when a cultural exchange program went to the Soviet Union for a concert." He leaned back in his chair and paused dramatically. "The other prints belong to Courtney Winthrop."

179

"But, they should be Nicole Chapman's. Who's Courtney Winthrop?"

"A spoiled rich girl involved with an anti-government terrorist group. The police arrested her seven years ago when the group planted a bomb under a police car. Luckily the police found it before it went off. They released and never charged her after her family got the best lawyers to defend her. The others involved spent time in prison." Bill shuffled the papers on his desk again. "She seems to have disappeared in the last few years. Now we believe she is involved with the White Moon. I just received a photo of her." He pulled it out of a folder and handed it to me.

I took it and stared at it. The hair was longer, but I recognized her from the picture the agency had showed me with Adriana Desi. "This is Nicole Chapman."

"No, Nicole died in a car accident. Her dental records identified her. She had been living on the farm in upstate New York for several years. She never left until the accident. We think Courtney had been using her identity. There is a resemblance as far as height, weight, hair color, and face shape. Not nearly the close resemblance Courtney has to you, but enough to get by." He handed me a grainy black-and-white photo of a woman who looked slightly like Courtney. He took the photos back and put them in the folder on his desk.

"Nicole Chapman was a high-school dropout, a follower, not the kind of person who could plan and execute anything on her own."

I remembered the reflection in the window the afternoon Adriana and I were shopping together, and something terrible occurred to me. "Courtney Winthrop is in Paris isn't she?"

Bill calmly replied. "Yes, we believe she is in Paris."

"Why wasn't I told this?" I asked angrily.

Bill sighed, exasperated with my naiveté. "It isn't necessary that you know everything about this case."

I sat back defeated. As a low-level, expendable agent, how did I ever become involved in this? Enraged by his treatment I sat up. "What do you mean I shouldn't know everything about this case? It involves not only me but also Adriana. Don't you care what might be happening to her? We don't know if she is still alive." I could feel my blood pressure soaring and my face burning.

Bill continued. "Desi may have known all along that Nicole, not Courtney, died in the accident. It is very possible that she has gone underground to join Courtney along with the other White Moon members."

"No, Adriana wouldn't do that, her singing career means everything to her, and I don't believe she knew that the person she thought of as Nicole didn't die in the accident."

Bill picked up a pen, twirled it in his fingers, and addressed me as he would a stubborn child. "Kathryn, you don't understand the minds of these people and how they operate. Everything is devoted to their cause, and no one or anything can get in their way." He dropped the pen on his desk. "I hope you haven't become so emotionally involved in this assignment that your judgment has been affected."

I ignored his comment about my emotional involvement. "My judgment tells me Adriana Desi is not part of the White Moon." I angrily thought how stubborn Bill was to not believe in Adriana's innocence and her dangerous situation. On top of that, I didn't need a lecture about the minds of the White Moon members.

Bill looked as if he was not going to discuss the issue with me any further. "Everything that can be done will be done. We have the resources. You are to return to the hotel. Is that understood?"

I nodded. I didn't have any option but to outwardly agree.

He stood, dismissing me. "I'll have a car take you back."

I knew they would make sure I returned to the hotel. As Michele had cautioned me: "no freelancing." But neither she nor Bill was going to stop me. If they couldn't find Adriana I would. But how?

✝

The driver let me off at the entrance to the hotel and waited until I was inside before driving away. I took some coffee up to my room; right now I couldn't eat anything. All I could think of was what Bill said about Adriana fleeing with the White Moon members. I didn't want to consider it, but now I had to. I crossed the room to the small wall safe. Inside were our passports. I remembered setting the combination when we arrived. Nervously, with shaking hands it took me three tries to open the safe. When the door swung aside I reached in and withdrew the folder. Inside were two passports—Adriana's and mine. Now I knew something had happened to her.

Feeling helpless I laid down on Adriana's bed burying my face in her pillow, holding it to me. Closing my eyes I relived the first time I saw her in the bookstore, and then sitting across from me during our dinner in the Italian restaurant in the East Village and, finally, making love together for the first time in her bed.

Desperate for action I got up off the bed. Lying on the bed and hanging around this room wouldn't help me find

Adriana. I had to do something. I had to have a plan. As I restlessly paced the room, the phone rang and I grabbed it.

"Kathryn? This is Suzanne Zantec. Have you heard anything about Adriana?"

"No, the police have been alerted, but nothing so far."

"Have you had dinner? I thought maybe you would like company."

I realized I hadn't eaten anything all day. Maybe it would help me to be with someone who cared about Adriana. "Could we eat here? The food in the restaurant is good and I want to be available in case there is any news."

"Of course. Is it all right if I meet you in an hour?"

"That would be fine." I called down to make a reservation and then changed my clothes while thinking how strange it was that Suzanne would have time for dinner tonight with a rehearsal in the morning.

†

I was already seated when Suzanne swept in. She removed her coat with a flourish and looked around her.

"Took me longer than I thought. I had to take a taxi since I let my driver go for the day. I'm not that far from here, but this time of the day the traffic is so bad. Jeffrey is still sleeping…I guess he has jet lag."

Suzanne put on her glasses and examined the wine list. "Let's get a bottle, what do you suggest?"

I glanced briefly at the wine list and pointed to a wine that Adriana had ordered when we ate here. "This is good."

The wine arrived and, peering at the menu, Suzanne put her finger on an item. "Let's see, this looks good. I wish my French were better." Sitting back, she ran a hand over her curls. "You know, if only I could figure out what happened with Adriana. She seemed so happy, even more so than in London last year." Removing her glasses she set her menu aside. "But this is a stressful profession, one never knows."

The waiter arrived to take our dinner order. I waited until he left and then asked. "You were with her in London?"

"Oh yes, *Aida*. A good performance, everything went so well. Great conductor we both liked working with, the reviews were excellent." She picked up her wine glass. "One night I saw Adriana going into a restaurant with someone who looked very much like you." She peered at me over her glass. "I guess you told me it wasn't you."

"Yes I did." Why did she bring this up again? "Was Adriana alone at the rehearsals in London?"

"Yes, I think so. It seemed that for some reason Maria couldn't come with her."

"Do you remember if something happened when you were there? A bombing in the Underground where some people were killed."

"Bombing?" Suzanne looked puzzled. "I guess there might have been. Probably the Irish."

Our meal arrived and Suzanne began eating with a hearty appetite. I sipped my wine and pushed my food around. Although flavorful, I had no interest in it." An idea occurred to me. "Suzanne, what was the name of the singer whom Adriana replaced?"

She put down her fork. "Elena Matlova. You don't think she had anything to do with Adriana's disappearance do you?"

"What was she like?"

Suzanne picked up her fork and rolled her eyes. "What the public thinks of as the stereotypical prima donna. Demanding, rude, self-centered, aggressive, and only concerned with her career. She was experiencing vocal problems as a result of singing roles unsuited to her voice, and a too strenuous schedule. Her husband is her manager. I think he was trained as a physician, but gave it up to manage her career."

"I just wondered."

"She was ruthless, but only in the opera house. I can't imagine her, or her husband, going to the extremes of doing anything to harm Adriana."

I remembered that the agency eliminated a stage designer in London as a White Moon suspect. But why? Maybe the agency had been wrong.

"Suzanne, who was the stage designer for your production of *Aida* in London?"

She closed her eyes in an effort to concentrate as she chewed a mouthful of food. "Let's see. Of course, it was Isabella Conti. Everyone loved the staging. Very traditional, but no monstrous staircases to navigate or live elephants on the stage." She added, "And a quite believable tomb in the pyramid."

Suzanne frowned as she picked up her water glass. "Certainly you don't suspect her of having anything to do with Adriana's disappearance?"

"Oh, no," I said hastily. "I just remembered Adriana saying she liked the production." Suzanne probably thought that in desperation I tried to blame Adriana's disappearance on anyone I could think of and she was right.

"Besides, she's back in the states right now. She's married to a conductor and they have one, maybe it's two, children." Suzanne reached for a piece of bread. "She's in big demand and I hear pretty busy."

Disappointed, I realized Isabella Conti did not fit the White Moon profile.

We continued our meal and I poured the last of the wine in Suzanne's glass. She lifted her glass. "I don't know what we are going to do. Of course they have an understudy, but she isn't really able to take Adriana's place for all the performances. Everyone wants to hear Adriana Desi in the role. Who could they get to come in now?" She shook her head, her curls flying. "I just don't know. They were so fortunate to have Adriana available."

Suzanne took a drink of her wine and blotted her mouth on her napkin. "I don't think they could replace *Don Carlo* with another opera at this late date. They will just have to find someone to sing Elisabetta. Poor Andre, he is beside himself as you can imagine. No one knows what to do." She sighed dramatically. "The whole cast is in turmoil."

I felt sick. Already Suzanne had decided the police wouldn't find Adriana in time for the opening night.

The meal ended. Suzanne tried to pay the check telling me that she had invited me. I insisted saying that she was my guest and signed my name and room number to the check.

We walked together to the entrance of the hotel. "I hope and pray she is found soon." Suzanne embraced me, got into a taxi and left.

As I turned back to the lobby I wondered if Suzanne thought Adriana had wandered off in a state of emotional or mental stress, not yet ready to perform again. If so she was wrong. Adriana had never been happier.

†

The thought of returning to our rooms depressed me, so I went into the bar and sat over a glass of wine while reviewing my conversation with Suzanne. The singer

Matlova might be a slim lead. From Suzanne's description of her, she seemed to be the kind of nasty person who would retaliate for losing her role in *Don Carlo*.

Then I remembered Suzanne had been in London when the White Moon bombing took place. Of course, the agency had eliminated everyone but Adriana. I dismissed any thoughts of Suzanne being involved. Singing filled her life so she would never get mixed up with a group like the White Moon.

In my bed that night I lay awake thinking about getting up and going to the restaurant to find the White Moon woman, then decided not to in case the agency called. I no longer cared what they thought of my actions, but I didn't want to miss any news they might have about Adriana. Finally in the early morning, I fell asleep with dreams of Adriana calling for me and I was unable to reach her.

†

The next morning when I awoke, I ordered coffee and a roll brought to my room. I drank the coffee, nibbled some of the roll, and tried to make sense of what had happened. I walked over and looked out the window at a gray, overcast day. Someone took Adriana and it had to be the White Moon. Looking at the clock, I saw I couldn't go to *Chez Simone* this early to find the woman. Another wild possibility occurred to me. What if the agency abducted Adriana to interrogate her about the White Moon's plans? No, Adriana had too high a profile with her upcoming performance at the Paris Opera for them to risk that.

I sank in a chair, picked up a magazine, threw it across the room, and then jumped up. I couldn't sit there any longer doing nothing. As I reached for my coat, the phone rang.

"Can you come down here? We'll send a car for you."

I recognized Bill's voice. He wasn't asking me but ordering me to go there. "Yes, of course. Is there any news?"

"The car will be there in a half hour."

I hung up, irritated by the secrecy. He could at least have told me something over the phone.

†

When I arrived at the agency a clerk took me to Bill's desk and asked me to wait. After a few minutes he came from a back room, smiling and carrying a mug of coffee.

"How about some coffee?" He sat down and took a sip.

"No thanks. I had some earlier." I waited impatiently.

He tipped his chair back. "Well, the police found a taxi driver late yesterday, bound and gagged, lying in an alley. He doesn't know anything except that he picked up a woman, who meets Desi's description, from your hotel in the morning. While he was at a stoplight a few blocks away, another woman opened the door and jumped in. There was a sharp pain in his arm and the next thing he remembers is that the police found him. The police think he received an injection of something to knock him out. They haven't found his taxi yet. No doubt it's abandoned in a garage somewhere."

"Doesn't this prove Adriana was kidnapped?" I asked eagerly.

Bill picked up his mug. "Not necessarily. This could be a ruse to make us believe that, or it may be totally unrelated to her disappearance."

"I think you might want to check on the whereabouts of Elena Matlova. She is the singer Adriana replaced. She may have tried to retaliate for losing the role to Adriana."

Bill made some notes on a piece of paper and left his desk to take it over to a woman working at a computer terminal. After a few minutes he returned.

"There isn't much else to tell you right now. Go back to the hotel and wait there. The driver will take you."

I continued sitting there. "Adriana was in that taxi. Why can't you believe someone abducted her? Why can't you find her? You call me down here and this is all you can tell me?"

Bill didn't reply but escorted me to the door.

✝

As the day before, the driver let me off at the hotel and waited until I was inside. At the desk I inquired about any mail or messages for me. There were none. I dutifully returned to my room and then walked back and forth between my room and Adriana's unable to concentrate on anything. Outside, although a light rain had begun to fall, I knew I had to get out of there. I put on my coat, took our umbrella, and went down to the street.

✝

Walking along I thought about my boasting to Adriana that I had devised a plan to prove her innocence. It had only amounted to following the woman from the bar and

189

I had promised Adriana I wouldn't do that. But now, everything had changed.

Despite the light rain, the streets were crowded, and once I saw a woman walking ahead of me who was the same height as Adriana and with the same long dark hair. I hurried to catch up to her, and when she turned to enter a café I saw her face. It was not Adriana. I stood there overwhelmed with disappointment and loneliness.

As the rain rolled off the umbrella I thought of our first meeting and how I had held an umbrella over Adriana as we walked together from the bookstore to my car. I recalled the night we returned to the hotel from *Chez Simone* and huddled in a doorway under the umbrella, with Adriana's arm around me.

The daylight had faded and, as I passed a bistro, I stopped to look in the window. It looked so warm and inviting, filled with people enjoying themselves. I remembered passing it the day we looked in the shops. Adriana had suggested we come back to eat there sometime. Would that ever happen?

I walked on and a few blocks later I entered the street with small shops and boutiques. I remembered exploring them with Adriana our first week in Paris. Looking in a shop window, I recalled the reflection behind me, which I now knew had to be Courtney Winthrop. Then I thought of something I might do to find Adriana. This fell into the category of a desperate plan.

After searching in two shops I found the items I wanted. I pointed to them. "I'll take these."

The young clerk removed them from the display and asked me. "You wish to try on?" She pointed to a fitting room.

"No." Impatiently I pulled out a handful of francs. Carrying my packages I hurried back to the hotel. If the agency had called me I planned to make up a story about going down to the restaurant in the hotel for something to eat.

The story wasn't necessary—no one had called.

I spent the next hour trying to read a book or leafing through a magazine while I waited to carry out my plan. At five the phone rang. I eagerly grabbed it.

"I just wanted you to know that Matlova is in Buenos Aires. She's doing a series of recitals, and we confirmed that she has been there nine days," Bill told me.

"Thank you." I hung up. The agency and police were accomplishing nothing. They were convinced that Adriana disappeared to join Courtney and the other White Moon members and she had not been abducted. They were wrong. Alone in a foreign city where I didn't speak the language, I felt helpless in finding her. I knew that my one connection to the White Moon, and only hope to find Adriana, had to be the woman she identified in the bar at *Chez Simone* that night. I would have to go ahead with what I now thought of as my desperation plan.

I flopped down on the bed to wait. By evening my growling stomach made me realize I hadn't eaten anything since the roll at breakfast. I called room service and ordered a sandwich, then as an afterthought, added in my halting French. "*Un double scotch et l'eau.*"

After I ate and threw down the drink, I changed my clothes, putting on my jeans and running shoes. I opened one of the bags containing my new purchases and pulled out a black wool, turtleneck sweater. From another bag, I took a short, black-leather jacket. I put them on and then got my suitcase from the closet, opened it and took the gun, a piece of cord, a bandana, and some other items from the false bottom. I checked the clip on the 9mm Beretta and then shoved the gun in my jacket pocket before adding a handful of extra bullets.

Before I left her room I picked up Adriana's robe, which was lying on the end of her bed, and held it to my face, inhaling her familiar scent. Then I carefully hung it in her closet and looked around at Adriana's possessions wondering if we would ever be here together again. I zipped up my jacket and left, quietly closing the door behind me.

Chapter Twenty-four

The evening rain had dwindled to a drizzle as I hurried along the sidewalk trying to suppress a feeling of panic. Adriana had been missing for almost two days, and neither the French police nor the agency could locate her.

I knew the agency thought she had run off to join the other White Moon members, but I also knew that Adriana's career and the performance of *Don Carlo* meant everything to her. What about the plans for our future together? And what about her feelings for me? I remembered Kitty accusing me of being too independent and never appearing to need anyone. She was wrong. It was not just desire. I knew I was falling in love with Adriana and desperately needed her. I did not intend to lose her now.

Outside *Chez Simone*, the restaurant where Adriana and I had eaten dinner together, I hesitated. Even though it was evening, I put on my sunglasses. It seemed a little melodramatic, but I looked too much like Nicole. Or was it Courtney?

Once inside, I hurriedly walked through the dining room and made my way past the crowd to a place at the bar. Anxiously, I scanned the bar looking for the woman Adriana had pointed out. Not seeing her, I ordered a scotch and water and tried to collect my thoughts. What if I had to come back here another night and perhaps another? All this time Adriana remained missing her life was in danger. How much longer would they keep her alive? Unfortunately, the woman who I now thought of as "the terrorist" represented my only link to the White Moon. I couldn't think of any other way to find Adriana.

I sat there dejectedly sipping my drink, wondering how long I would have to sit in the noise and cigarette smoke of the bar waiting for the terrorist woman to show up. I ordered another drink and when I looked up I saw her. Her head was down as she rudely elbowed her way to the end of the bar where she signaled for a drink, and began talking to the woman seated next to her. She wore the same black-leather jacket, though not as new as mine, and had the same short, careless haircut. Evidently the women knew one another as they carried on an intense conversation. As I watched, they seemed to be arguing about something.

I peeked over the rim of my glass as another woman came in and joined them. Suddenly, the terrorist woman jumped up, said something in anger to them, and started toward the women's room. I waited a minute, put some money on the bar for a tip, and moved over to examine the *Absinthe Ducros Fils* poster on the wall outside the door. The door of the women's room opened and she came out. When she started past me I grabbed her arm, spun her around, and put the barrel of my gun to her back.

194

"I want you to walk slowly to that rear door." She tried to protest in French and pull away. I gave her a shove with the gun trying to control my anger. "I know you speak English and you understand what I am saying." Adriana once told me Nicole did not speak French so she must have spoken English with this woman. "I will shoot you right here. I can be out the door and gone in all the confusion. You will be dead."

I pushed her ahead of me and we went out the back exit to a shadowy parking area. Suddenly she struggled trying to spin around and face me.

"Courtney?" She looked at me more closely and her eyes widened. "No, you are not her. Let me go." She struggled to break away.

I brought my gun down sharply on her head. It hit the side with a crack and bounced off. I thought she would fall down, but she briefly staggered and was quiet. I could see blood seeping out around her hair. I ignored it.

"That's better, where's your car?" She blinked and nodded toward an older Renault in the nearby parking area.

I waved my gun toward the car. "Get in and drive. I want you to take me to Adriana Desi. Don't pretend you don't know what I am telling you." I pushed the gun toward her. "You are expendable. If you don't take me to her I will get rid of you and find someone else to do it. Do as I say and I won't harm you." My voice shook with anger. My only hope of finding Adriana depended on this woman and I no longer cared what it took to do it.

As she drove, she furiously ground the gears on her car. Once, she put her hand to her head, now bleeding freely, and angrily muttered in French what were probably obscenities. I kept my gun on her and, as we drove further, a light rain began to fall. When it came down increasingly harder, the vision of the road became blurred. I took off my sunglasses and ordered. "Turn on your windshield wipers." When she didn't respond I roughly pushed my gun against her temple. "You heard me. Do it now!"

Grumbling more of what I assumed were obscenities directed at me, she finally complied. The wipers flopped ineffectively back and forth, smearing the windshield.

Driving further we appeared to be on the outskirts of Paris, where the homes were set back from the road, protected by tall trees, heavy bushes, and tangled undergrowth. She pulled over to the side of the road, pointed to a large house ahead, and sullenly announced. "I can't go any further. They will hear and see me if I go in the drive."

"Get out." I motioned toward some nearby bushes. When we reached them, I took a coil of thin cord from my pocket. "Turn around." I tied her hands. "Lie down." She resentfully complied and I tied her ankles to her hands. "Keep still, you will eventually be found."

As a further precaution I took a bandanna from my pocket and tied it over her mouth.

By now my jeans were damp and my hair soaked. Holding my gun in my right hand, I carefully made my way along the row of bushes to the back of the house. I had a small flashlight, but feared that if I used it someone could see the light from the house. In the darkness, I could just make out long, glass, double doors in the back of the house leading to the garden. Trying to enter there would be taking too much of a chance of someone inside seeing me. Over on the side of the house was a large wooden door set between two scraggly overgrown shrubs. I waited, listening and watching. No one appeared to be in the yard, so I quickly crossed to the door and tried the handle. Locked. Taking some tools from my pocket I started working on the lock. Although I was not very adept at this skill, the lock was an old one and not too challenging. After I spent a few minutes of fumbling with it, the lock clicked. I slowly opened the door and cautiously stepped into a dark hallway.

As my eyes became accustomed to the darkness, I could see a staircase to the left leading down to the basement. On the right was another door. I inched it open, hoping it wouldn't make any noise. Peering in, I could see a large kitchen. On a table in the center of the room were strewn dirty plates, glasses, and a half-empty bottle of red wine. Another partially opened door let in some light, while a weak light on the wall on the other side of the room provided more faint light.

Hearing distant voices, I quickly closed the door and looked toward the basement stairway. I got the flashlight from my pocket and turned it on. The stairs were old and dirty, and as I descended some emitted faint creaks when I stepped on them.

At the bottom of the stairs, I took a deep breath and swept the flashlight around the cold, musty, damp room, where the surfaces of the walls were crumbling in places, littering the floor. The basement appeared to be a storage area for abandoned items consisting of boxes, ancient trunks, pieces of discarded furniture, and some old windows in a pile. Apprehensively, I directed the light to the corners of the room. To my relief, the collection of junk, creeping spiders, and cobwebs appeared to be all that was down there.

I decided to go back upstairs. If the White Moon had brought Adriana to this house I had to find her. Carefully climbing the stairs, I opened the door to the kitchen and waited, listening for voices. Not hearing anyone, I stepped into the kitchen and swiftly crossed to the other door. Slowly opening it, I found myself in a gloomy hall. A large mirror hung on the wall facing me, and in it I saw a ghostly image of a woman in black with light hair and a determined look. Startled, I realized I saw my own reflection. Ahead, a broad winding carpeted staircase led upstairs. At the bottom of the staircase I paused, listening. The bedrooms would be up there and maybe the White Moon fanatics held Adriana in one of them. As I put my hand on the banister and started to climb the stairs, I felt something pushed into my back.

"Stay right there and put your hands in front of you. This is a gun in your back."

I immediately thought of turning quickly and trying to overpower her, but my gun was in my pocket and her gruff voice gave the impression of a big woman. I decided it would be best to go along for now.

"Turn around and get going over to that room." She shoved me ahead of her toward a heavy paneled door that was slightly ajar, letting a faint light spill into the hall.

When we came to the door, she reached out and pushed it open, prodding me with her gun as I stumbled into the room, blinking and trying to keep my balance.

We were in a room intended to be a den or library with heavy, leather furniture, and bookcases along one wall. To my left, a short, stocky woman wearing a worn black-leather jacket and short, black boots stood with her arms crossed, glaring at me. At the far end of the room, a large desk with a lamp on it provided the only light in the room. A woman sat at the desk with her face in the shadows.

The woman commanded. "Bring her over here."

My captor pressed her gun in my back and as we crossed the room to the table, the woman rose to her feet, stepping into the light.

"Well look at this, my twin." With contempt in her voice she added. "At last we meet."

In the lamplight I could see my resemblance to Courtney, but I could also see the differences. Although slightly heavier than I and with longer hair, the real difference lay in her face. There would never be any love nor kindness expressed there.

"So, this is Adriana's new little lover. Isn't it pretty strange how she managed to find someone who looked like her lost love?" She smirked. "So how is Adriana in bed? I found her drearily possessive."

Enraged, I lunged at her, but my captor grabbed my arms and jerked them behind me. I struggled as she tightened her grip, sending intense pains shooting up to my shoulders.

Courtney looked at me with disdain and ordered, "Check her pockets."

My captor removed my gun and flashlight, held them up, and looked at Courtney. "How about this—a gun. What do you suppose she was up to?"

Courtney laughed. "Who knows? Better hang on to her tightly. She has a gun so she's a danger to us."

I twisted in my captor's grip, which only sent more pains up my arms.

Courtney sat down and leaned back in her chair putting her face back in the shadows.

"When I first met Adriana in the park with that dog I was walking, I thought she might be attractive enough to pursue, but when I found out she was an opera singer and often traveled abroad, it was perfect. As her companion, I had an ideal cover for the places I traveled to for our missions."

Helplessly I struggled to get free and attack her. "How could you have treated Adriana as you did?" I shouted. "Didn't you care about her at all?"

Courtney grinned at me. "It was fun for awhile, but eventually I was afraid Adriana was going to realize what I was up to. London was a close call after the bombing and then we had a little disagreement back in New York. I decided it was time to leave Adriana by dying in a tragic car accident. Poor stupid Nicole. We gave her a chance to take the car, to escape from the farm, after she overheard our talk about the successful bombing in London and our future plans. She was so naïve to think she could do anything to stop us."

I strained in her grip as my captor held me tightly. "You killed her!"

"Unfortunately there was something wrong with the car. The brakes I believe." She leaned forward into the light of the lamp with a smug smile. "When it came to politics, Adriana was hopeless. There was no way she would ever be interested in the political causes I live for. Now, with you on the scene, I can't afford to keep Adriana around." She laughed. "I'm afraid this will be her last act."

Suddenly I had hope. Adriana was still alive.

The woman standing across the room wearing the leather jacket giggled, and Courtney turned to her.

"How about a car accident with the two lovers?" She gestured toward me. "Take her to the basement and tie her up. Be careful, she's clever. Don't let her get away, whatever it takes. I have plans for her."

While being led away she called out to me, "By the way, the dog wasn't mine. It belonged to my former lover. I later heard it was run over by a car." Her maniacal laughter followed me.

The woman with the gun marched me down to the basement. While in the den, I had taken a look at her and, as I suspected, she was much taller and stronger than I.

†

"Get over here and lay down." She tied my hands behind me. I tried to spread my fingers and arms as much as possible like the agency taught me, but she did a good job. Next she tied my ankles together and then tied my arms to one of the posts in the basement. After she finished she stood glaring down at me, her broad face red with anger.

"Just when things were going good for us you had to come here, meddling and upsetting Courtney." She drew back her foot and aimed a kick at my head. I managed to roll away and her foot landed on my side. As she climbed the stairs I felt a sharp pain in my ribs and gasped for breath.

I lay there for what might have been an hour or more, cold and numb from my cramped position on the hard damp floor. Although my leather jacket had partially protected me from the rain my legs and hair were soaked. My drifting thoughts returned to happy memories of the time when Adriana and I, together, made plans for our future. Reluctantly, I pulled my thoughts back to my present situation as a prisoner in a basement in Paris. I knew the White Moon held Adriana here, and I had to find her before they harmed her.

On this side of the house an outside yard light let in a weak light through the dirty, high, basement windows. Seeing the faint outline of some storm windows leaning against an old trunk, I maneuvered my body around the post until my feet were near one of the windows. I stretched as far as I could and kicked my feet. On the third try I heard the sound of breaking glass. I lay still, waiting for someone to appear and investigate the noise. But the house had thick walls to deaden the sound, or else they had all gone up to the bedrooms, thinking I was securely imprisoned in the basement. When no one appeared, I used my feet to try sliding a piece of the broken glass over to my hands. Eventually I was able to grasp a piece with my fingers and I started working on the rope. Several times I dropped the piece of glass, and once I cut my hand. Just as my fingers were becoming too numb to hold the glass, I felt the rope slacken. I pulled my arms apart, worked a little more and finally the rope gave way. I sat there rubbing my hands trying to restore the circulation. At last the feeling returned enough for me to untie my feet.

I carefully arranged the rope so I could slip into it if I heard someone coming to check on me and then painfully got to my feet. My side hurt where the woman had kicked me, my head ached, and my knees and arms were stiff from the cold and dampness.

I realized that without my gun I would have no weapon if I encountered the group upstairs. Looking around me I saw an old, dirty, wooden box pushed against the wall. Fearful of what it contained I carefully opened it to see an assortment of rusty tools, and rummaging through them as quietly as I could, I selected a hammer.

I slowly climbed the stairs and waited at the door to the kitchen, listening for voices. Only silence. Hopefully by now they had all gone to bed. I moved forward and cautiously pushed open the door, carrying my rusty hammer.

Everything happened at once. I heard screams, bursts of gunfire, and an explosion. I stepped back feeling myself falling while desperately trying to grasp the railing along the wall as I tumbled backwards down the basement stairs.

Chapter Twenty-five

I opened my eyes to the glare of a bright light shining on me. Two men bent down, grabbed my arms, pulled me to my feet, and dragged me up the stairs. I saw they wore uniforms, but with my head throbbing and the intense pains shooting through my left shoulder, I couldn't think clearly.

We emerged onto the lawn where all around were police cars, ambulances, lights and a crowd of curious onlookers being held back by the police. As I dangled between the arms of two policemen a man stepped forward.

"She's one of ours. I'll take her," Bill said.

He led me over to a black Citroen, opened the back door, and motioned for me to get in. Someone else sat in the car.

"Is this your idea of returning to your hotel and letting us handle this?"

Startled, I looked into Michele's face. But not the Michele I knew in New York. Instead of being severely pulled back, her hair was down around her shoulders and she wasn't wearing her glasses. Her open, tan, suede coat revealed a very attractive body in a closely fitting black sweater and black slacks in place of her usual tailored suits.

I shook my head and blinked. "Michele, how did you get here?"

"As soon as I saw the report on the fingerprints, I caught the first flight over here. With Courtney Winthrop in Paris, I knew you were going to be in trouble." She looked at me with concern. "I was partly responsible for letting you come over here on this assignment."

I made a painful examination of my body. My head still hurt, there was blood from a cut on my forehead, and running my right hand over the back of my head I discovered a large bump. I couldn't raise my left arm and thought I might be sick to my stomach.

Michele had a slight smile on her face. "In that outfit, the police thought you were one of the White Moon members and almost hauled you away. I don't think you are too badly hurt, but we will have you taken for an examination."

She took a tissue from her pocket, and carefully pushing back my damp tangled hair, dabbed the blood on my forehead. "It seems you fell down the basement steps when the shooting started."

"Shooting?" With my heart pounding I looked over at the house, afraid to ask. "Adriana. Have you found her?"

"They located her in an upstairs bedroom. She doesn't remember anything after she got in the taxi yesterday morning. She probably received the same drug as the taxi driver. They have taken her to the hospital for observation, but she appears to be fine."

That was all I cared about. I lay back in the seat and closed my eyes.

Michele continued. "Our special police found the bodies of three women, assumed to be White Moon members. They were in the library and although they had exchanged gunfire with the police, each died by a single bullet to the head, execution style. We think one of them shot the others and then herself."

I opened my eyes. "Was Courtney Winthrop among them?"

"The bodies haven't been identified yet, but very likely she was one of them. We found another woman in the bushes in the yard, tied up and unharmed. She claims some terrorist woman abducted her from a bar. We will interrogate her later."

Despite my pain and confusion I took a deep breath and then let it out. With Adriana safe and her innocence proven, I looked at a Michele I didn't know existed.

The car door opened and Bill reached in. "Come on, let's get you over to that ambulance, and make sure you're okay."

Michele put her hand on my arm and I saw a look on her face I had never seen before. "Kathryn, I am so relieved you are all right. If anything had happened to you," she paused and pressed my arm. "Never mind, get going."

Accompanied by Bill I walked unsteadily across the lawn, through the lights, blaring police radios, and arriving reporters. Another ambulance pulled away, and even though the occupants were beyond help, the sirens screamed in the night.

†

I sat next to Adriana's bed in the hospital. "Are you sure you're all right?" I looked anxiously at Adriana. With her pale face against her dark hair on the pillow, she appeared exhausted.

"Yes I am, but look at you, my darling. They tell me you were at the house, trying to rescue me, and almost died in the gunfire." She reached for my hand and held it tightly.

With a touch of pride I replied, "I'm fine." I fingered the bandage on my forehead. "No stitches, just a butterfly. My shoulder is only sprained and the bump on my head is nothing. No concussion."

Adriana sighed with relief. "Kathryn, this is all so confusing. Why did those women kidnap me? Were they White Moon members?"

With difficulty I told Adriana about the person she thought of as Nicole. "Adriana, the woman you knew as Nicole Chapman was really a woman named Courtney Winthrop, leader of the White Moon. She was using Nicole's identity. Nicole never left the farm in upstate New York until she died in the car accident. Courtney arranged the accident to end her relationship with you. She had been using you as a cover to travel abroad and direct the bombings and other terrorist acts. Courtney was afraid you would find out she was still alive, so she decided to get rid of you."

"How I regret becoming involved with that woman," Adriana said bitterly.

I understood how she felt. "We all have regrets about someone in our past. You and I are together now." I had one last thing to tell her. "Courtney died in the shootout with the police."

Adriana nodded. "So, now she really is dead. It is all so hard to understand."

We sat together in silence.

"Adriana, darling!" Suzanne Zantec stood poised in the doorway holding a bouquet of flowers in her hand, a look of concern on her face.

I released Adriana's hand, stood and moved aside as Suzanne rushed toward Adriana, dropping the flowers on the bedside table and gingerly embracing her.

"How dreadful to be kidnapped and held for ransom. We think they were going to approach the opera house and demand the ransom, and of course with the performance coming up, the company would have paid. You will be able to perform won't you?" She looked anxiously at Adriana who attempted a bright smile.

"Yes, I am being released in a few hours."

Suzanne sank into the chair that I had vacated. "What are things coming to? Kidnapping opera singers. I can't stay too long. Jeffrey is waiting downstairs. I told him from now on, until the performances are over, he has to be with me every minute."

She turned to me and ordered, "Kathryn, don't you leave Adriana's side."

I noticed Adriana trying to suppress a smile.

"No, I won't." It was an order I would have no trouble fulfilling.

"Suzanne, this was just a small group of criminals, and the police have killed or arrested them all. We don't have to worry now." Adriana's gaze fell on the flowers lying on the bedside table. "How lovely, thank you. I will have them put in water."

Clutching her purse, Suzanne got up from her chair. "Although this has certainly upset us all, it is big news in the opera world." She beamed. "All this publicity is really helping the ticket sales."

Giving Adriana a brief kiss on the cheek, she started for the door and then turned back, dramatically putting her hand over her heart. "Thank God you are safe and *Don Carlo* will go on."

After she left I resumed my place in the chair next to Adriana, and she again took up my hand. "Kathryn, when the performances here in Paris are over, why don't we take a short vacation together before returning to New York. Would you like that?"

"It would be wonderful. I would love to." I looked at her affectionately, so grateful that we were together again after her rescue.

She pressed my hand. "I know just the place. I think we will like it."

Chapter Twenty-six

Everyone declared *Don Carlo* a wonderful success and the opening night a special one in the opera world. The powerful performances by everyone in the cast would have assured it, but Adriana's magnificent performance, and the publicity surrounding her disappearance, resulted in sold-out performances. As I had predicted, Adriana singing Elisabetta's aria in Act IV, *Tu che le vanita conoscesti del mondo*, brought a long, standing ovation at every performance.

The typical overly dramatic, excessive newspaper headlines screamed "Diva Kidnapped" or "Opera Star Abducted By Petty Criminals For Ransom."

†

The Paris Opera arranged a reception following the final performance of *Don Carlo*. The cast and a select group of dignitaries, high profile donors, musicians, and others deemed worthy, attended.

When I arrived in the grand ballroom, Suzanne Zantec hurried over to me shrieking. "Kathryn, you look fabulous!"

I wore the black dress I had bought in New York, and with the low neckline, I added my Mikimoto pearls. This seemed to be the event to wear them.

Suzanne's ample breasts overflowed in a tightly fitted, red-satin creation with a plunging neckline.

"Good evening, Kathryn." This, with a slight bow, from a solemn Jeffrey. Evidently Suzanne gave me the seal of approval.

"Adriana is exquisite tonight." Suzanne sighed and we all looked across the room to where Adriana stood talking with a large group gathered around her. She looked elegant in an emerald green gown, which set off her alabaster skin and dark hair.

"Oh, just think what would have happened if those kidnappers had succeeded. I might have been next." Suzanne clasped Jeffrey's arm. "Thank God I have you to protect me." Jeffrey managed to look both proud and embarrassed.

The official release from the police announced that a small group of criminal elements had decided to take advantage of the publicity surrounding Adriana's appearance at the Paris Opera, and had kidnapped her for ransom.

Suzanne peered at my forehead. "That cut has healed up very well."

To my dismay and embarrassment, the agency fabricated a story explaining that the cut on my forehead from my fall down the stairs in the shootout had happened when I fell while jogging. The agency decided that no one should know I had been at the house that night. When I grumbled about this, Adriana had lightly kissed my forehead. "Never mind, darling, I know you are not clumsy. Not at all."

Suzanne pouted. "We never got to go out to dinner together, and now you and Adriana are leaving Paris." Before I could reply she turned her attention to scanning the room.

"Look, Jeffrey! There's that famous French pianist. He's so handsome." As I watched Suzanne drag Jeffrey away, I realized that I would miss her, drama and all. Fortunately, we would all be together again in April, at the Met in New York, for a performance of *Il Trovatore*.

After Suzanne left I wandered over to an empty table and sat down.

"May I join you?" I looked up to see a slim woman with a blond pageboy, stylishly dressed in an electric blue, off-the-shoulder gown, who was holding a glass of champagne.

I motioned for her to sit next to me.

"Are you in the cast?" She spoke with a French accent.

"No, I am with Adriana Desi."

We both looked over to where Adriana stood talking to the conductor and the tall imposing Italian bass who sang the role of King Philip.

She nodded. "I see. She is a very talented woman and also beautiful. What extraordinary fortitude to go on and perform so wonderfully, and so soon after the awful kidnapping ordeal."

"Yes, I agree," I said, wondering to whom I was talking. I started to ask her name but she had more questions.

She frowned. "I still don't understand why those criminals would kidnap an opera singer. Where did they think the Paris Opera would get money for the ransom?"

I shook my head. "I have no idea." As I hoped, she changed the subject.

"Are you related? I seem to remember a cousin who traveled as her companion. And last year there was another woman with her."

"I am not related."

She was probably trying to guess exactly what my relationship to Adriana was. "It must have been a terrible experience for you when she disappeared, not knowing what had happened to her, and if she would be found unharmed." I saw her waiting expectantly for my response.

I remembered my feelings of panic, despair, and helplessness. "It was something I never want to relive."

She looked me over appraisingly. "Can I get you a drink?"

Before I could reply, a tall woman with short dark hair and a determined expression approached our table and glowered down at my new companion.

"Come over here with me, there's someone I want you to meet," she ordered.

The woman sitting at my table stood up, smiled, and shrugged. "Excuse me." They departed.

"Kathryn, what did Jeanne have to say about the performance?" Adriana sat down in the recently vacated chair.

"Jeanne?"

"Yes, dear, the woman you were talking with, Jeanne Charbonneau. She is a music critic and gave me a glowing review on opening night."

"Well, tonight she tried to pick me up."

Adriana laughed. "I certainly don't blame her."

"She didn't get very far. Her girlfriend came over and snatched her away." I looked fondly at Adriana. "It wouldn't have gone anywhere. I have someone I love very much."

She looked at me tenderly. "And I love you too, Kathryn." We stood gazing at each other, oblivious to everyone around us. Adriana put her hand on my arm. "You look so lovely tonight. Let's go back to our hotel. I am exhausted."

"Fine with me." I looked around. "Is it all right that you leave?"

Adriana suppressed a yawn. "I have circulated and chatted with everyone. Come, dear."

As we left the ballroom Adriana took my hand. I looked over and saw the music critic watching us with a smile while her friend glared.

✝

With my help, Adriana removed her beautiful gown and draped it over a chair next to her bed. "I'm too tired to hang it up, it can wait until morning." Smiling, she turned to me. "Let me help you with your dress." She unzipped it and I stepped out and threw it on the chair. I unclasped my pearls and dropped them on the bedside table.

We finished undressing and Adriana took my hand leading me to her bed. "Say those words again, Kathryn."

We lay down and I pulled the covers over us. I held her hand and lightly kissed her temple, whispering, "I love you, Adriana."

She sighed. "Oh, you know I love you, Kathryn." She closed her eyes and I felt her hand relax in mine as her breathing slowed and she fell asleep. I soon joined her.

213

†

The next day we were starting to pack, preparing to leave for our trip in two days. Adriana had gone down to the lobby to pick up her mail and a newspaper. When she returned to the room, I lay on her bed leafing through a magazine.

"You are supposed to be packing." Adriana gave me a playful slap on my leg with the newspaper and then sat on the edge of the bed with an envelope in her hand.

"Look, Kathryn, I have another letter from Maria."

When the news of Adriana's rescue from the kidnapping attempt appeared in the press, Maria had been on the phone nonstop. At first she had blamed herself for not coming to Paris with Adriana to protect her, but seemed relieved when Adriana assured her she couldn't have done anything, and things were fine now.

Adriana tore open the envelope and sat there reading the letter.

"Maria is happy that the performances were so successful." She turned the sheet over. "Oh, listen to this, Maria has decided that they will permanently move to Florida. It seems Sophia loves it there. But, Maria is concerned that she will be leaving me alone in New York." She looked at me.

"Tell her Sophia comes first."

Adriana nodded. "Yes, a good idea." She read further. "And guess what?"

"I can't guess."

"Well, Renata and Marco have a friend, a widower who is a few years older than Maria, and they have been seeing one another." She looked puzzled. "What do you think that means?"

"Probably dining out at supper clubs and long walks on the beach." I added, "I hope he is Italian."

Adriana frowned at the page. "Yes, I believe he is." Then she looked up, began laughing, reached over, and tousled my hair. "You are terrible."

I grabbed her arm and pulled her down to me. "Yes, I know. What are you going to do about it?"

The letter fell to the floor as Adriana put her arms around me and tugged lightly at the sleeve of my sweater. "Take off your clothes."

I struggled out of my sweater as Adriana pulled it off and tossed it aside. She unbuttoned her silk shirt, shrugged it off, and unhooked her bra, exposing her lovely breasts. The rest of our clothes fell in a pile on the floor.

Adriana took me in her arms, our bodies pressed closely together. Our lips met and she moved my mouth down to her breasts. We made love long and slow, savoring each other completely, never wanting this moment to end. As a lover, Adriana combined the passion of her operatic roles with the gentleness of her personality, and I think, even as a scientist, I satisfied her.

We lay together in the tangled sheets and I stroked her hair as she took my hand and held it. "When did you first know you loved me?" she asked softly.

"When I listened to your recording. Before I ever met you." I remembered my passionate feelings that night, alone in my apartment, as I listened to her voice.

"Kathryn, I have loved you since we met, but never knew for sure how you felt about me. I can't tell you how happy I was when you agreed to accompany me to Paris."

Adriana turned to me. "Kathryn, there is something I want to ask you... please don't feel you must make a decision now."

I propped myself up on my elbow and looked down at her. "What is it?" I asked with concern.

"Now that Maria and Sophia are moving to Florida ..." she hesitated. "I was wondering if, when we return to New York, you might want to come and live with me."

I lay back on the bed, pulled her closer, and felt the warmth of her body against mine. I brushed the hair away from her face and smelled the delightful scent of her shampoo. "I don't have to think about it." I kissed her cheek. "The answer is yes. I would love to."

Chapter Twenty-seven

I entered the Parisian café and stood adjusting my eyes to the subdued lighting. Michele sat at a secluded table in the rear of the room with her back against the wall. I had never met her before in public, only at the agency with her in charge behind her desk. When she summoned me to a meeting, it surprised me to learn that she hadn't left Paris after Adriana's rescue.

I sat across from her and waited until our glasses of wine arrived. "I didn't know you had stayed on here."

"I have quite a bit of vacation time that I've never used. Once our business here was concluded, I decided to stay and see some of Paris again." She looked embarrassed. "I even attended a performance of *Don Carlo*."

"You did?" As I tried to comprehend this she continued. "I very much enjoyed it. Adriana was exciting. She is a talented singer and an excellent actress."

I waited, but evidently she had nothing more to say about the performance. I briefly wondered if she had gone alone. Then my thoughts turned to the White Moon. "Michele, have you found out who committed the execution shooting of the White Moon members?"

She didn't immediately answer my question, but sat for a moment and then reluctantly replied. "Kathryn, I have to tell you that we did not find Courtney's body with the others. It appears she did the shooting, no doubt afraid they would talk if the police captured them. Somehow, she escaped."

I was stunned and afraid for us. "She got away?"

Michele added confidently. "I assure you we will find her."

"But you said three bodies were found. I only saw two women besides Courtney."

"There probably was another woman upstairs guarding Adriana."

I noticed Michele no longer referred to her as Desi, but now called her Adriana.

"What about the woman you found in the bushes? Could she tell you anything?" I wondered what she had to say about her abduction from the bar, and if it would be linked to me.

Michele shifted uneasily in her chair. "She hung herself in jail, very embarrassing for the police, as well it should be."

"Michele, how did the agency know where to find Adriana?"

"We were alerted when Courtney Winthrop entered France, and informed when she arrived in Paris. After Adriana's abduction, with our contacts and resources, we were able to trace Courtney and the White Moon members to the house outside Paris."

"If you knew Adriana was there, she could have been hurt in the raid." I said indignantly, still upset that they had risked her life.

Michele pushed back her hair and picked up her glass. "Kathryn, don't forget we still did not know if she had fled to join the White Moon members or truly was abducted by them. When our special police force found her in an upstairs bedroom, it became apparent that she was being held captive and still being drugged."

Michele took a drink and set her glass down. "We now know Adriana is innocent of any involvement with the White Moon. Of course, it didn't help that we had a disobedient agent interfering. You came very close to being killed in the shootout."

I humbly mumbled, "I know." I really wanted to say, But I wasn't killed and how was I to know the agency was doing anything to find Adriana?

For a moment I wondered if this could be a dream as I sat there in a café in Paris, drinking wine with Michele, who was casually dressed in slacks and a green sweater, which matched her eyes. Still without her glasses and with her hair down around her shoulders she had a surprisingly youthful appearance.

I took a sip of my wine. The time had come to tell her. "Michele, I'm leaving the agency. I don't want to do this work anymore." I waited uneasily for her reply.

Michele ran her slim fingers down the stem of her wine glass, wearing what I thought of as her stern, agency expression. "Kathryn, no one ever really leaves the agency. No one. However, we are prepared to give you a leave of absence."

"I don't plan to go back to the lab either. I'm going to stay with Adriana and travel with her."

Michele leaned forward, her hand on her chin. "Amy will miss you. She was very pleased with your work in the lab and your help in solving the theft problem."

Amy? I always suspected that the agency and the lab had some connection, but here was Michele on a first name basis with Dr. Lan. So they knew one another. Could they possibly see each other outside of work?

Michele sat back in her chair, her expression no longer stern. "Kathryn, I hope you have thought this out, but if you ever need anything or if your circumstances change, promise you will come to me. The agency will be keeping track of you. There will always be an assignment waiting for you."

I saw again that her eyes were really green. "Of course, thank you, Michele." Although grateful, I didn't think it would ever be necessary to accept her offer.

We sat in silence looking at one another and then, appearing resigned to my decision, she sighed, drank the rest of her wine, and stood. I had an impulse to embrace her, but instead I got to my feet and we shook hands. She held my hand for a moment and then turned away.

As I watched her leave the café I experienced a brief moment of loss, but now my life had a new direction.

Chapter Twenty-eight

I put my arm up to shield my eyes from the sun. Adriana lay beside me in a lounge chair in the shade at the edge of the pool in the enclosed garden of our hotel. We were on the Island of Capri for a short vacation before returning to New York.

Adriana closed the book she was reading, written in French, the biography of a female opera singer who lived in early nineteenth-century Paris. Before we left Paris, she had discovered it in an old bookshop and enjoyed reading passages to me. From the time of her rescue, until the successful conclusion of the performances of *Don Carlo*, Adriana's manager had been continually on the phone. The U.S. newspapers and magazines all clamored for an exclusive interview with her, and one late-night talk show tried to line her up for an appearance when she returned to

New York. All this publicity had stimulated frenzied ticket sales for her Met appearance in late April.

Even Suzanne Zantec had shared in the publicity, giving interviews to the press describing how she lived in fear of a kidnapping herself, and how dangerous the life of an opera singer had become.

I turned my head to the right to look at Adriana, rested, relaxed, and as lovely as ever.

She put her hand over mine. "Kathryn, where should we have dinner tonight?"

"I don't know, I guess I haven't thought about it."

"What about the restaurant we went to our first night here?" She turned her face to me, shielding her eyes with the other hand.

The first night. What a wonderful, exciting memory. After strolling together through the narrow streets and alleyways hung with flowers and browsing in the shops, we ate outdoors by candlelight in a restaurant with a vine-draped verandah in a garden setting. We had an exquisitely prepared meal with excellent wine and gracious service. Afterwards we planned to walk to a view overlooking the Mediterranean, but Adriana pointed out that our room had a balcony, which also had a stunning view of the sea.

Returning to our room we fell to the bed in a tangle of arms and legs, each anxious to please the other, and our lovemaking became feverish and passionate. When our lips met we could not get enough. With our bodies held closely together we desperately clung to one another. I felt a shiver run through me as she ran her fingers down my body and her hand trailed up between my thighs. The other two nights had been just as memorable, but this one remained special. The thought of that night and a possible repeat made me weak with desire.

"I'd love to go back there, let's do it."

Adriana withdrew her hand and turned her body slightly to face me. "Kathryn, do you think you will regret not going back to the laboratory? Will you miss the work?" she asked with concern in her voice.

"It isn't even in my thoughts anymore." Financially well off with the inheritance from my parents, I had a new plan for my future. "Several years ago I started writing a mystery novel. It seemed to have promise according to my writing instructor, but something came up in my life and I put it aside. I have been looking at it again and now I'll have time to work on it. It will be good for me."

After rethinking the story I made the honest decision to have the two women become lovers. It would mean the addition of several chapters and a rewrite of the ending. I would have them move into the heroine's old Victorian home to share the rest of their lives together, not to save on expenses. I didn't care if it made the book harder to place. I had to write what I felt.

"Oh, Kathryn, how exciting. I have always loved reading mysteries." She looked at me eagerly. "I know you will be successful and we will have a good life together, not all work. When we travel we will try to have some times like this for ourselves."

While feeling the warmth of the sun on my body, I looked out at the terraced hills, brightly colored flowers, and cloudless blue sky. Then I looked at Adriana, reached over, and pressed her hand. "There isn't any more I want, except for one thing."

"What is that?" Adriana looked at me with a troubled expression.

"That we always be together."

She smiled with relief. "We will be."

We lay there in silence for a few minutes until Adriana sat up and looked down at me with a seductive smile. "I think we both have had enough of the sun. If we go back to our room now we could have some time together before dinner."

I immediately leaped up and began gathering our things together. We climbed the steps of the terrace to our room. I unlocked the door and Adriana entered ahead of me, but part of the way into the room she stopped abruptly and let out a cry. Close behind, I collided with her and then looked across the room.

The closed window shutters kept out the afternoon sun, but there in the shadowy room, in a chair and pointing a gun at us, sat Courtney Winthrop.

Adriana gasped. "Who are you? I thought you were dead?"

I stepped in front of Adriana. "This is Courtney Winthrop, the woman who was using Nicole Chapman's identity when you met her."

"You didn't die with the others that night?" Adriana asked in confusion.

"Adriana, Courtney shot the other women and then escaped."

Courtney jumped up and came toward us waving the gun. "Enough. Adriana, tell this new lover of yours to shut her mouth." She jammed the gun into my side.

As I stumbled backward Adriana put her hand on my shoulder to steady me and moved in front of me. I could feel her trembling, not with fear, but with anger. "You are despicable. I can forget what you did to me, but don't you dare harm Kathryn."

Courtney sneered. "Adriana shut up. You're not in charge here and this isn't one of your dramatic opera performances. Stand over there, both of you, and keep your hands where I can see them."

She pointed her gun at Adriana. "You were useful for awhile. A great cover for my travels. I even entertained the thought that I might convert you to our beliefs, but you only cared about singing. It all became very tedious." She chuckled. "You know, I always disliked opera."

The afternoon sun sank and the room grew dimmer as Courtney rambled on, her talk becoming more disjointed and detached from reality.

"Our bombings have been successful." She paused and frowned. "But there is competition from other groups. They'll see, we will overcome them and prevail. Now we have plans for a new attack. Everyone will know us, fear us." She waved her gun to emphasize her points.

As Courtney continued her tirade, I tried to estimate the distance between us, determined that after everything she had been through, Adriana would not die here at the hands of this woman. If I could rush her and try to get her gun it would give Adriana time to escape, no matter what happened after that. I decided to stall for more time and then make my move, hoping to catch her off guard.

Without the breeze from the sea or the overhead fan, the shuttered room had become stifling. A bead of perspiration trickled down my cheek, and close in front of me I saw Adriana's back was damp. My legs ached from standing still for so long.

I took several deep breaths to calm myself. "What's the purpose of harming us? If you do that the police will find you. As it is now you're free. You can still get away."

As much as I hated to say it I added, "We won't try to stop you." I tried to adopt a soothing tone as I waited for the right moment to make my move.

With her face flushed from the heat and dripping perspiration Courtney leveled her gun at me. "I've wasted enough time. I'm afraid there is going to be a tragic murder and suicide taking place here. The older woman finding out her younger lover has been cheating and then ending it all."

I heard a crash from the direction of the balcony and the sound of a single gunshot. I pushed Adriana to the floor covering her body with mine. I waited in the silence that followed and then looked down at Adriana. She didn't move. Gently, then urgently I shook her. She opened her eyes and looked up at me.

"Kathryn, are you all right?"

"Yes, but what about you?"

"I think I had the breath knocked out of me."

Turning, I looked over to see Courtney's body sprawled on the floor and kneeling over her, Michele. Shakily I stood and helped Adriana to her feet.

"Michele, I thought you went back to New York." As soon as I said it I thought it wasn't a very appreciative greeting for a person who just saved our lives.

Michele rose to her feet still holding her gun. "Not while Courtney was at large. We have been expecting her to come after both of you. When I got word that she had followed you to Capri, I came right over."

I took Adriana's arm. "Adriana, this is Michele, a special agent with the International Intervention Agency."

At this moment the door to our room burst open, and Bill and two other agents rushed into the room.

Bill knelt over Courtney's body. "She's dead." Then he looked around. "Is everyone okay?"

"Yes, thanks to Michele." Adriana smiled at her. "She was very brave and saved our lives."

†

That evening, Bill, Michele, Adriana, and myself sat together at dinner. Although not our special restaurant, which Adriana and I were saving for our last night in Capri, the restaurant had a lovely view of the harbor. We all were relaxed after a few glasses of wine and an excellent meal of seafood delicacies.

Bill looked like a typical American tourist in a gaudy, bright-print shirt, and I wondered if maybe it was part of his cover. Michele, dressed simply but attractively, smiled at Adriana who looked especially elegant wearing her amber earrings and necklace with a sleeveless, low-cut black top.

Adriana returned her smile. "I am so grateful to you for saving us and destroying the White Moon."

Bill signaled for the check. "Unfortunately, another group will take their place."

Michele sighed. "How true." She paused. "But how courageous you were to go on with the performances of *Don Carlo* after the ordeal of your abduction."

"Singing is my life. It is because of your bravery that Kathryn and I are here."

Michele made a slight gesture of dismissal with her hand. "Part of my job." She leaned forward. "I do want to attend your performance at the Met in April. I hope there will be tickets available when I get back."

Adriana looked pleased. "I will obtain two tickets for you, so you can bring a friend. Kathryn will get them to you."

I wondered whom Michele would bring. It would be interesting, and for some reason I didn't think it would be a man. Would it possibly be Dr. Lan? I stifled a yawn. Right now I was more interested in ending the evening and returning to the hotel before I was too exhausted to do anything except sleep. Earlier that evening, after the trouble in our room, the agency arranged for us to move to another room, which promised an even more spectacular view of the sea from the balcony.

Finally, Bill stretched, yawned, and paid the check. At last the evening was coming to an end. We all stood and said our last goodbyes.

Later that evening Adriana held me in her arms as my head rested on her shoulder.

"Kathryn, there is something I want to ask you." She hesitated, searching for the words. "Do you think, sometime, if it would be possible, maybe we could get a little dog?"

In the darkness I smiled and took her hand. "I think we could arrange that."

Epilogue

Santa Fe, New Mexico, 2006

I typed a passage into my computer, deleted a word, and hit *Save*. The time before dawn in the cool darkness was my favorite time to write. Now, as I looked out the window, the sun was peeking over the horizon. Across the room a bookcase held my last five mystery novels. I had created a series that featured an attractive, yet smart, lesbian detective whom mystery fans were eager to read about. My last book, *The Coach Bag Caper*, had been especially successful, receiving rave reviews. The author's photo on the book jacket showed a slim, smiling woman, with medium-length blonde hair standing, with her arms crossed next to an old MGB. It had been Adriana's idea for me to pose with my MGB.

"It has a wonderful memory for me, the first time we were together." She smiled. "You were so shy."

I returned her smile. "Great idea. Better than the one my publisher suggested with me staring pensively into the distance, with my hands jammed in my jacket pockets."

I shut off the computer, walked in my bare feet down the tiled hall to our bedroom, and stood in the doorway.

Adriana sat up smiling. "Good morning, Kathryn." She stretched and yawned as our little dog, Minnie, stood wagging her tail.

For the past six summers, when the Met was not performing, Adriana had appeared with the Santa Fe Opera. Two years ago we bought a home here to live in when we were not in New York. I crossed the room and sat on the edge of the bed, rubbing Minnie's back.

I watched Adriana look fondly at Minnie. "She feels very important since her picture appeared in *Opera News* magazine.

The March issue featured Adriana at home on what they described as her ranch. In a photo taken on the patio, Adriana, wearing a filmy low-cut blouse, held Minnie on her lap. The little dog looked quite appealing with her fluffy white fur and coal-black eyes. The interviewer asked Adriana about her dog's name.

"I wanted to name her after one of my roles, but Mimi, Violetta, Tosca, they all die in the end. Then I thought of Minnie in Puccini's *La fanciulla del West*."

"Oh, yes." The earnest young man interviewing her added, "*The Girl of The Golden West.* One of your signature roles."

Another picture showing Adriana at the wheel of our jeep caused much laughter between us since Adriana didn't have a driver's license and I did all the driving. In the most stunning photo, Adriana wore tight jeans, cowboy boots, and a light-blue work shirt with the sleeves rolled up, and unbuttoned enough to show some cleavage.

Minnie jumped down and I took her place on the bed next to Adriana. She turned to me. "How is the new book coming, dear?"

"I'm writing about the White Moon." Michele and Amy, whom I still thought of as Dr. Lan, had flown down in July for the opening night of Adriana's performance. Five years ago, Michele became Chief of Operations when Dr. Caldwell retired, and seeing them had given me an idea for the book.

Adriana rose up on her elbow and asked with a troubled look. "The White Moon?"

"Yes, I want to expose that kind of horrible terrorist group."

Adriana fell back. "A good idea." As we lay there together, I thought about how our relationship had began with a contrived meeting and been grounded in deceit. We had overcome this and fallen in love. Ten years later, we were even more in love, and each day we looked forward with hope to our future together.

Adriana broke the silence when she hesitantly said, "Kathryn, do you remember that night in Paris, in my room, when we…?"

She didn't need to say more I remembered the night vividly. I pulled off my pajama pants and sweatshirt, throwing them to the floor. Adriana kicked the covers aside and with my help removed her pajamas. She held out her arms and we embraced. Our lips met in a passionate, lingering kiss, and our bodies moved together. Even after all this time her familiar body was still so exciting.

"My darling Kathryn."

"My lovely Adriana."

We held each other as the sun rose over another day of our life together.

THE END

About the Author

Natalie London

Natalie London served three years with the Peace Corps in Thailand and many years as the manager of a hospital chemistry laboratory. She is a Master Gardener, Certified Beekeeper, and plays the French horn, recorder, and flute. Natalie, her partner, and their calico cat live in southeast Wisconsin.

Other Books from Affinity eBook Press

The Circle Dance by Jen Silver Jamie Steele has moved to another town trying to forget the heartbreak of losing her lover of six years. Sasha Fairfield, finds her thoughts taken up with her ex-lover and thinks she wants Jamie back. Follow this captivating romance as love dances through the lives of these women to its surprising conclusion.

Take Me As I Am by JM Dragon & Erin O'Reilly When Jo Lackerly and Thea Danvers meet, an unexpected friendship develops, proving a catalyst for both women to change their lives irrevocably. Follow them on a journey of discovery that will have your heart smiling, blood boiling, and senses entangled in a wonderful romance.

Carved in Stone by Jen Silver Join the characters from Starting Over and Arc Over Time in this final book from the Starling Hill trilogy. Ellie Winters thinks she might be going mad when the ancient queen wants a proper burial for herself and her consort. *Carved in Stone* has romance, adventure, a treasure hunt, and a happy endings for all, living and dead.

Anywhere, Everywhere by Renee MacKenzie Gwen Martin's life in the Ten Thousand Islands area changes irrevocably when Piper Jackson comes into her life. Without trust, can the budding relationship between Gwen and Piper survive? Or will the answers to the questions continue to haunt them?

Venus Rising by Ali Spooner Levi Johnson arrives at Venus Rising, an exclusive lesbian only tropical resort in the Virgin Islands and finds more than she expected—a sizzling hot love triangle. Torn between her attraction to both women struggles to choose the right woman to share her life.

The Devil's Tree by Ali Spooner Torn between her love for the pack and her need to find what's missing in her life Devin Benoit travels to New Orleans. Will the previous happenings at the Devil's Tree help or hinder Devin in the fight of her life, and the life of Tia, the woman who now owns her heart?

The Beggars' Coppice by Erica Lawson Edda Case is a woman in crisis who discovers that things are not as they seem. Is it truly a message for her from beyond the grave or is something more sinister taking place? Can Edda solve the mystery of *The Beggars' Coppice*?

Locked Inside by Annette Mori How much does the power of love matter to someone who must overcome obstacles far greater than most people face in a lifetime.

Line of Sight by Ali Spooner Sasha and her lover Kara are back. Continue the thrilling adventures of this couple from the Sasha Thibodaux series.

Requiem for Vukovar by Angela Koenig Requiem for Vukovar continues the Refraction series and the exploits of Jeri O'Donnell and her partner, Kelly Corcoran. In an epic siege largely ignored by the wider world, Kelly, who was prepared to give up comforts and certainties when she became part of Jeri's nomadic life, encounters more than physical danger. Her ability to maintain her core integrity is assaulted by the inevitable ugliness of war. For Jeri, the true battle is confronting her attraction to violence as she struggles against losing herself in the exhilaration of combat.

Against All Odds by JM Dragon From award winning and bestselling author JM Dragon, with significant updates by, Erin O'Reilly comes an original tale of romance where everything seems to be stacked against two women whose destinies bring them together. Life however takes a twisted path setting both Steph and Louise in directions they never thought possible. Will love win out against all odds or will love be forever lost?

The Settlement by Ali Spooner The outpouring of love and friendship toward Cadin helps her on her path to healing and learning to trust her heart to love once again. Join bestselling author Ali Spooner on this sensational journey that ends with a heartwarming romance.

Once Upon a Time by Alane Hotchkin Raven only wanted to escape the blows that life had dealt her. She longed to be on the open sea and free. When she came upon a beautiful young girl sitting alone in the middle of a meadow, little did she know that her destiny would be changed forever. Will they become the pawns of the ancient vision or will both paths lead to the same port of destiny? Find out it in this exciting high seas adventure that will capture your imagination.

Asset Management by Annette Mori Follow the twists and turns to the explosive conclusion. Not everything is black and white. There are many shades of gray and sometimes it's difficult to decipher who is good and who is evil. No one is all virtue or all malevolence, but sometimes love helps us rise above.

Do Dreams Come True? by JM Dragon How do two people who really shouldn't get on end up in a relationship? Find out in this deliciously ordinary romance.

Return to Me by Erin O'Reilly Will Salvation bring just that to Ellie, allowing her to find peace and happiness again, or will it have her questioning all that she believes in? A wonderful romance cloaked within an intriguing mystery.

Arc Over Time by Jen Silver This wonderful romantic continuation with the characters from *Starting Over* ties up loose ends. But the question is—does everyone have a happy ending? A must read.

The Presence by Charlene Neal Can Rebecca and Kayleigh overcome ghosts from the past and their own insecurities, or will a presence from the past tear them apart?

A Walk Away by Lacey Schmidt Sometimes chance brings you to the right person to help you resolve some of your baggage, and you learn to like yourself a little more. Kat and Rand are smart enough to recognize this chance in each other, but they also find that there is a catch to every opportunity—walking toward something is always walking away from something else.

Possessing Morgan by Erica Lawson The investigation has barely begun when Andrea becomes the target of a nearly fatal hit-and-run. But was it really aimed at her? Can she and Morgan find the common ground they need to solve the case and stop the attacks, or are the gaps just too wide to bridge?

Twenty-three Miles by Renee MacKenzie This is a story about community, and how it comes together in dangerous and devastating times. When you don't know who to trust, you better have friends who will rally around you. Will Talia and Shay find the answers they need to the mystery of the murders on the parkway, or will justice be elusive? Will they survive their quest for the truth?

Reece's Star by TJ Vertigo Under Faith's guiding, loving hand, will Reece successfully traverse the rocky road of emotion and embrace the positive changes in her life? Or will she panic and be unable to control that Animal part of herself? Will she take that next step to declare herself fully capable of love and devotion? This third installment in the popular series that began with *Private Dancer* continues the passionate and often hilarious romance of Reece and Faith as they both grow in love and in trust.

Confined Spaces by Renee MacKenzie Corporate politics, complicated romance, and long distances conspire to keep Andie and Kara all boxed in. Can love triumph despite the Confined Spaces?

Cowgirl Up by Ali Spooner Ride along with the MC2, for boot scootin', butt kickin', dirt eatin', rodeo adventures, with a love story thrown into the mix.

If I Were a Boy by Erin O'Reilly Will Katie and Helen be able to make a life together work or succumb to doubts and the pressures of family? This story will fill you with the thrill of passion and the tenderness of love.

The Chronicles of Ratha: Book 2 A Lion Among the Lambs by Erica Lawson Can Jordana believe in herself like her Noorthi sisters do? Only then can she fulfill her destiny as The Chosen One. Follow the colorful cast of characters in this action-packed adventure sequel as they traverse the galaxy. Of course, nothing ever goes smoothly when Jordana is involved.

Terminal Event by Ali Spooner Will the killer be caught or continue to evade authorities? Can Tally and Blair's budding romance survive the possibility? Read this intense murder mystery romance and find out.

Love Forever, Live Forever by Annette Mori Fate intervenes and puts Nicky directly back into the path of her first love, Sara, and the corresponding events send her into a tailspin. Now she must decide—who will be the person she ends up living with and loving forever?

The One by JM Dragon *2015 GCLS Winner for Romance, Intrigue, and Adventure. The One* is a romance with everything, love, intrigue, misunderstandings with a happy conclusion—the only question—who gets the girl?

Reflected Passion by Erica Lawson Through a mirror, Françoise embraces life anew, while for Dale it is a powerful awakening, forcing her to discover not only her sensual nature, but the inner strength she possesses.

Flight by Renee Mackenzie Some lives will be lost and others changed forever when the sisters' lives intersect. Will they be consumed by the wreckage, or will they be able to pick themselves up and take flight?

Starting Over by Jen Silver Book 1 of the Starling Hill Trilogy. There's a mystery afoot—whose royal resting place is disturbed at Starling Hill? All is revealed in this classic romance of simmering passions, anguished loss, and the wonder of love.

E-Books, Print, Free e-books

Visit our website for more publications available online.

www.affinityebooks.com

Published by Affinity E-Book Press NZ LTD
Canterbury, New Zealand

Registered Company 2517228

www.ingramcontent.com/pod-product-compliance
Lightning Source LLC
Chambersburg PA
CBHW060547260626
47161CB00003B/1085